City Bear has been around the block a few times, but his true nature keeps drawing him back to something no man ever could build or invent except out of time spent alone with his Creator.

Returning from the metaphysical realm with the name bestowed upon him by his spiritual guide, Dr. Andy McCabe leads us on a tour de force of healing practices through the use of a teaching tale both original and reminiscent of *Aesop's Fables*, the maxims of Lao Tzu, the parables of Jesus, and Hasidic stories from the nineteenth century.

While staying true to the oral tradition of storytellers the world over, McCabe has invented a new prose genre, self-help fiction, insisting in *The Gifted One* that his readers really can be the individuals they always wanted to be without pretending, and then showing them how to do it.

Richard A. Biagioli, Ph.D.
Clinical Psychology
University of Connecticut
Westfield, New Jersey

Enlightenment is only the beginning! *The Gifted One* will leave finger prints on your mind.

Karen VonMerveldt-Guevara
German trained M.D. and
Alternative Healer
Sedona, Arizona

The Gifted One is an invitation for anyone who has a desire to take a journey within to heal an ailing self. Clear and inviting style with lessons that will last a lifetime.

Peter M. Kalellis, Ph.D.
Author of *Letting Go of Baggage,
A Journey Through Life's Challenges.*
Westfield, New Jersey

Dr. Andy McCabe's unique story telling ability takes you gently into life's deeper mysteries…the journey and fulfillment of one's soul… and leads you into awareness's and realizations that support, teach and share in the style of the ancient masters. Deep…Thought provoking, compelling, helpful and cathartic, could not put it down…

Maria Elena Cairo
Healer and Intuitive, Trained
in Aztec & Mayan Shamanism,
Phoenix, Arizona

A guidepost for life. *The Gifted One* is a must reading for people who are on the crossroads of their lives. A powerful, fun and insightful read.

Rowena Francisco, M.D.
Adult/Adolescent/Child
Psychiatrist
Chester, NJ

The Gifted One takes the reader on an adventure of self discovery that introduces him/her to the higher wiser self. Readers will be inspired to realize new and positive life skills. Intriguing! I couldn't put it down.

Kathleen Carrera
Transformational Coach
Washington State

The Gifted One:
The Journey Begins

Andrew Aloysius McCabe

BALBOA.
PRESS

A DIVISION OF HAY HOUSE

Balboa Press books may be ordered through booksellers or by contacting:

Balboa Press
A Division of Hay House
1663 Liberty Drive
Bloomington, IN 47403
www.balboapress.com
1-(877) 407-4847

Because of the dynamic nature of the Internet, any Web addresses or links contained in this book may have changed since publication and may no longer be valid. The views expressed in this work are solely those of the author and do not necessarily reflect the views of the publisher, and the publisher hereby disclaims any responsibility for them.

The author of this book does not dispense medical advice or prescribe the use of any technique as a form of treatment for physical, emotional, or medical problems without the advice of a physician, either directly or indirectly. The intent of the author is only to offer information of a general nature to help you in your quest for emotional and spiritual well-being. In the event you use any of the information in this book for yourself, which is your constitutional right, the author and the publisher assume no responsibility for your actions.

Any people depicted in stock imagery provided by Thinkstock are models, and such images are being used for illustrative purposes only.
Certain stock imagery © Thinkstock.

ISBN: 978-1-4525-0045-4 (sc)
ISBN: 978-1-4525-0157-4 (e)
ISBN: 978-1-4525-0046-1 (hc)

Library of Congress Control Number: 2011900169

Printed in the United States of America

Balboa Press rev. date: 12/1/2011

Cover artwork by Nathaniel Sharkey

Dedication

The Gifted One: The Journey Begins is dedicated to Charles Maher, Psy.D., Full Professor, Graduate School of Applied and Professional Psychology at Rutgers University. Charlie, as his students know him, was my advocate, teacher, and coach. He guided and inspired me to work at a level beyond which I thought I was capable and without him, I would not be Dr. McCabe today.

Acknowledgements

The creation and completion of *The Gifted One: The Journey Begins* involved a number of people whose assistance, support, guidance, and talent I wish to recognize.

Dr. Alan Burghauser, has my gratitude as he opened the door for me to begin my work with Native Americans.

To Meredith Mazak and Sylvia Krieger you have my thanks for typing the manuscript.

For their patience in reviewing and editing the manuscript, I would like to thank: Patrick McCabe, Psy.D., Rosemary Albach, Erin McCabe, Jeff Wilbert, Jodi McCabe, Mary Alice McCullough, Ed.D., Joseph Babaco, Richard Biagioli, Ph.D., Peter Kalellis, Ph.D., Karen Von-Merveldt-Guevara, M.D., Anthony Amabile, Marykate Gonzales, Psy.D., Mark Kitzie, Psy.D., Dr. Rowena Francisco, M.D., my wife, Deborah Wozniak McCabe, M.D., Joel Pierson, Editor, Balboa Books, as well as my colleague and literary mid-wife, Sherry Folb.

My special thanks to Dr. Sonia Choquette for reading the manuscript, as well as her words of encouragement and support.

My sincere thanks and appreciation to Maria Elena Cairo for allowing me to use her channeled mantra "All of Us are One" in the final chapter.

For their friendship, as well as their assistance in helping me gain an appreciation for, and a novice understanding of the Hopi culture, my thanks to Joseph and Janice Day, Tsakurshovi Trading Post, Second Mesa, Hopi Reservation, AZ.

I'm most grateful to Steven Zazenski, artist, for his assistance in helping conceptualize the book cover, and to Nathaniel Sharkey, graphic designer, who created the front cover and bear paw trademark.

For her professionalism, skill and guidance with this project, my thanks to Kathleen Carrera, Transformational Life Coach.

For Joanne Bruno, J.D., Vice President for Academic Affairs, New Jersey City University, thank you for your career support.

For their patience, interest, and skill in taking this project from manuscript to book, my thanks to the staff at Balboa Books: Colin Boyle, Brian Martindale, Joel Pierson and Valerie Deem.

And most of all, my thanks to Mary Ethel and Andy Sr., mom and pop, who provided me with the most wonderful and supportive family anyone could hope for: brother Jim, sister Mary and brother Pat.

Contents

Backstory

The Gifted One has its origin in a chance encounter with Father Theophane, a Trappist Monk, whom I met at St. Joseph's Abbey in Spenser, Massachusetts over twenty years ago. He was that rare individual who lived his life in two worlds: the one that we see, and the world of the Divine. He was who he was ... *with no pretending*. The few hours I had the honor of spending with him influenced my thinking forever. I hope he is smiling on my work from his place in heaven.

In 1993 I was seriously ill and knew that my fate lay in the hands of the surgeon operating on me. Prior to the operation, I was so weak I couldn't speak. I could, however, hear those around me and when someone said something unkind or nasty about a co-worker or doctor, it drained the energy from my body. I remember thinking, *please stop, say something nice, or don't speak*. My illness provided me with the opportunity to understand the power of our words.

When I awoke after the operation, three messages kept repeating in my mind like a silent mantra for the entire day. They were: be kind to my first wife, Alice; the only thing that matters is kindness; and finally, there is not enough time to do all the good things that need to be done. Like the clacking of freight train wheels, those messages had a mind of their own. I couldn't stop them and went to sleep listening to their silent repetition. When I awoke the next day, the plug had been pulled on the tape recorder. I know that life-threatening event and those messages have influenced this book.

Finally, my friend, Ed Norton and I were motoring my sailboat from Raritan Bay to a dock in Jersey City. I was leaning back against the lifeline when it broke and I fell backward into the ocean—about a mile off Sandy Hook and two miles from the Verrazano Bridge. In the second it took to go from sitting to falling, I remember thinking, *don't get knocked out, and then, you haven't finished the book.* After Ed fished me out, I wondered, *why didn't I think of my family and friends? Why the book?* The recognition that this book is something I had to finish has been with me since that autumn day.

Chapter One

My name is Theophane.
I am a gift bearer.

Subway Surprise

The doors of the PATH train banged open at Thirty-third Street, and the momentum of the crowd moved me toward the stairs that led to the street above. I remember thinking that New York in February could depress the Good Humor man, when I felt the tug at my sleeve.

I'm always paranoid in Manhattan, so my alarm bells went off when I felt the touch. I turned and looked directly into the bottom of his chest. Like a child looking up at a tall building, I tilted my head back. My first thoughts were: *So tall! So thin! A giant scarecrow with a man's face!*

Then the odor invited itself in; he smelled like the New Jersey Turnpike near the Linden Oil refinery, like rotten eggs. It made me gag.

I was ready to pull my sleeve from his skeleton grasp when I looked into his eyes. They startled me. There were no pupils; each held a sparkling green iris. They looked more like emeralds than eyes. Overpowering. I couldn't look away or think, but then, regaining my composure, I thought—*is this really happening?*

My mind began to scan everything I'd ever experienced, and like machine-gun fire, questions whizzed through my consciousness. *Why is the giant so thin? Why hasn't he spoken? Why can't I move?* Followed by my warped mind whispering—*maybe he wants to tell you your fly is open? That you're losing altitude?* My thinking works that way. Making fun of things, especially scary stuff, takes the edge off.

In a plaintive yet jovial tone, he said, "Friend, may I, a weary traveler, trouble you for some coins, so that I might purchase a cup of liquid refreshment?"

Whew! He wants a handout. Give it to him and get out of here. Maybe this is starting to make sense.

When I put my hand in my pocket, I remembered that I deposited my last quarter in a parking meter in Hoboken. I only had tokens for the train.

Why not? Give him a dollar and have it over with. But when I went through my wallet, the smallest I had was a five.

The seconds that had passed since he tugged at my sleeve seemed like minutes.

His eyes! They're so weird. My thoughts kept ruminating about his eyes. I decided to give him the five.

I handed it to him, but he didn't take it. Then I said, "Here you go; get something to eat with your liquid refreshment."

He held out his hand and I placed the bill in his palm. He put it in the right-hand pocket of his wrinkled black raincoat.

He had been carrying a stained brown shopping bag in his right hand and what looked like a short, metallic club in the other. He had put the bag down to take the money. As he did, he put the club in his left pocket. After he put the money away, he turned his palms toward me facing up and bowed his head.

"Holy moly," I murmured to myself and thought he was going to start to pray, but instead he took a step back and gave me the space I needed to escape.

I was halfway to the stairs when I heard, "Mac … Mac … Come back … please … I beseech you!"

Beseech? Who says beseech in the New York subway? I could only think of clergy and milk-crate philosophers proclaiming the end of the world.

"Mac, I have a gift for you," he said.

After I heard him call me Mac the second time, it registered! *Does he call everyone Mac, or does he know my last name is McCabe?*

He didn't have to offer a gift. I was already on my way back. Sister Martina, my fourth-grade teacher, was the last person I can remember saying *beseech*. I think it had something to do with one of the kids who kept blowing his nose and disrupting the class. She was losing it. Beseech was the final warning before she went over the edge to the place where nuns go to reclaim their sanity. *Beseech* was serious. Like when a cop says, "*Please* step out of the vehicle."

As I walked toward the mystery man, I believed I didn't want, or need, whatever it was that he thought was so important. What I needed to do was lose fifty pounds, get my blood pressure out of the stratosphere, find a new job, make more money, repair my strained family relationships, and most of all, learn to relax. For a long time, I felt like a gerbil on a wheel and I wanted desperately to escape.

"Mac! Just a few seconds of your life … I have it here for you … I have been waiting to give it to you for a long time."

Why me?

They can pick me out in a crowd. I could be wearing Hell's Angels colors with ripped dungarees and they'd still know I was a soft touch. It's a curse.

On my way back, I saw him rummaging through his bag.

"I have it here. I know it is here. Just a moment! Ah! Yes! I have found your treasure."

When I returned he handed me what appeared to be a ledger. Like everything else about him except his eyes, the book looked worn—no, more like *ancient*. As if many fingers had caressed its texture before mine and, in doing so, left minuscule deposits of oil that had darkened the fabric. The cover, if my guess was correct, had become a repository for the DNA of everyone who touched it—if it wasn't a scam.

My internal alarm bells were still sounding and I wondered, *maybe I'm on Candid Camera. Maybe a Gypsy was going to pick my pocket (or already had).* At the same time that I checked to see if I had my wallet, I noticed the odor was gone. Instead, there was a fragrance of freshness, and I wondered if someone had turned on an exhaust fan. It smelled like the forest after a morning rain shower and before the heat of the day. *Too much input. Not enough answers. I'm on overload.*

When I looked into his eyes, he said, "My name is Theophane. I am a gift bearer. My job—or I should say my vocation—is to travel the world and reward kindness and compassion wherever I find it. The world is such a mess you know, so much evil ... but there is also great good. I am here to recognize those who deserve to move to the next level, and you have passed your first test for consideration."

Test? What was he talking about? I gave him a handout? No big deal!

"You could have walked away when you remembered that you put your last quarter in a parking meter. It became more difficult when you realized that the smallest bill you had was five dollars. It was here that you earned your gift. You were no longer afraid of me. My smell and clothes did not matter. You thought I looked hungry and you presented your gift knowing that there was nothing I could do for you in return."

I interrupted him. "What do you mean consideration?"

"For the privilege of allowing me to help you change and your assistance in helping to heal our ailing planet."

I was working on processing his answer when he continued. "The book I have given you is what you need. What you really need. I know about your health, your job, your family, your book, and your money problems."

How does he know all this?

Then he said, "As you suspected, the book is very old. It is much older than you imagine."

He smiled, closed his eyes, bowed his head toward me, and turned away. I stood there in shock as he took the metallic club from his pocket and unfolded it into a cane ... a white cane with a red tip.

My last memory of him was watching the bones of his shoulder blades undulate under the worn, thin fabric of his coat, as he walked with the tentative gait of the blind, his cane acting as a scanner, while his right hand held his bag of treasures.

I was on my way to see Mel, my prospective publisher. I had spoken to his secretary so many times that all I had to do was say, "Hi, Sandra," and she'd recognize my voice. I usually joke with secretaries and I try to remember their names. This approach is not limited to secretaries; it's directed toward people who I sense want to laugh if you give them the slightest reason. Maybe because when I had jobs that were boring, I was always looking for a laugh, something to make the time pass on my way to a paycheck.

During one of our conversations, she told me that Mel liked to call himself "Mel the Magnificent." She found that hilarious because he combed his thin strands of hair from his left temple up and over to cover his ever-widening bald spot. Apparently, it was incongruent to her that anyone with his hairstyle could call himself magnificent.

Magnificent or not, if it meant selling my book at a great price, I'd call him magnificent or Uncle Mel, whatever it took, as long I got the money I felt the book deserved, as long as I didn't have to do anything I couldn't share with my mother.

My appointment with Mel had lost its importance as I gripped the book.

"Get hold of yourself," I mumbled, "The guy is probably schizophrenic, or maybe he's a con man." *Where's the con? I had given him the money before he gave me the book. Maybe the con hasn't unfolded yet? Maybe he pulls this act a hundred times a day and lives in a mansion in Scarsdale ... maybe his wife is a credit card junkie and he does his act on the way to work to make extra money ... maybe he showers at work and puts on an Armani suit.*

My inner voice of reason was screaming: *you jerk! Throw the book away and get on with the day. You have a meeting with Mel.*

I passed a trashcan and made the decision. I couldn't throw it away. I kept thinking of his eyes. They were unlike the eyes of any blind man or woman I had ever met. They radiated joy, peace, and a profound sense of compassion and understanding. His eyes held a secret I wanted to know.

After he walked away, I stood there looking at the book cover. It had the texture of linen. As I flipped through its few pages, it seemed to tell a story. I turned to the inside cover and found a raised, gold-colored fleur-de-lis pattern that appeared to be made of some kind of very thin metal I didn't recognize. In a pocket, like a library card holder but smaller, under the fleur-de-lis, was the top quarter of what looked like a business card. I removed the card and observed how the upper right- and left-hand corners had the same pattern as the inside cover of the book. In the middle it read, in gold leaf print, The Gifted One. The lower left-hand corner advised By Appointment Only, and the lower right-hand corner listed a phone number. There was no address. Unlike the book, the card looked new.

The six-by-nine-inch book contained only three pages of text, followed by three pages of handwritten signatures and dates. The book was bound with three tiny cords tied in bows that went through holes in the covers about one inch from the left side. The holes were evenly spaced at the top, middle, and bottom of the book, and the bows allowed pages to be easily added or removed.

I looked up in anticipation of running after him, but he was gone. In the direction that he walked, there was only a platform and no stairs—the station was empty. I needed to sit down and make some sense of all this. My watch read 7:13 AM. My 8:00 appointment with

Mel had taken a back seat to the book. I was intrigued. I wanted to see what it was about. I'd figure out an excuse to tell Mel's secretary. I wanted to find a place to steady myself with some strong coffee, and learn about my supposed treasure. I suspected it wouldn't take long.

Across the street from the subway exit, I found a sandwich shop that had tables in the back. I ordered coffee and took a seat against the rear wall. I sat facing whoever came in, and it made me feel like a cop. I was nervous and needed to see the arriving customers. For some reason, seeing them enter made me feel safe. I turned to the first page. The black print was perfectly executed in an ancient, precise hand, like something that might have been copied by a monk in a moldy, candlelit abbey in the Middle Ages. It read:

Thank You for Your Gift

By now, you know my name is Theophane and it has been my task to travel the world and find people who will be brought to the next level. To do so, they will be taught to overcome their life challenges and heal themselves in preparation for their work.

Yes, I am blind. It is not a trick. My father and his father, and the fathers before them, for centuries, were blind. We have been using this book for eons and the names of those who accepted the challenge are listed on the last three pages and signed in their own hand. We hope to add your name to the list.

I turned to the signature pages, which looked older than the text, read the names, and said to myself, *"Wow!"* Some of them were written in Greek or Latin, and for those, the English translation was printed in black fountain pen next to each. Some of the names went back to antiquity, and I remembered them from Latin classes in high school. Others were unknown to me, and some were modern historical greats from the eighteenth, nineteenth, and twentieth centuries. *This couldn't be.* There were three additional blank signature spaces.

If you accept your training and pass, you will be asked to add your name to the list. Whether you accept or not, keep this book safe. If you choose not to embrace this challenge, a messenger will be sent to retrieve it. If you accept your mission, you will give the book to your teacher, whose name is identified on the card placed inside the cover.

A list is kept of everyone who has passed the first test and been offered our gifts. Some accept the challenge; some refuse. Many of those who chose to move to the next level have changed the course of human history. You have an opportunity to become one of them.

You have many questions about me and I trust the following will answer most of them. As a young man, my father told me that our lineage goes back to the Golden Age of Greece. He said that our forefathers believed our blindness could be traced to the legend of Tiresias who was known throughout Greece for his wisdom.

Supposedly, Zeus, the king of the gods, was arguing with his wife Hera about who enjoyed lovemaking more, the male or the female. As the story goes, Hera had changed Tiresias into a woman after hitting copulating snakes with a stick. No one is exactly sure why his action made Hera angry. However, later he was changed back to a man after leaving the copulating snakes alone the next time he saw them. Since he had experienced both being a male and a female, he was consulted and asked to settle the dispute. He responded, "Why, the female, of course. Nine times more than the male!"

Hera was angered again. Why? Tiresias revealed woman's greatest secret when he said, "Of ten parts, a man enjoys one only." Hera thought his response was impious, as it was not the response she had wanted; so in punishment, she struck Tiresias blind. Zeus, feeling responsible for his wife's action, but not being able to restore Tiresius' sight, decided to give him the gifts of insight, prophecy, and understanding.

According to my father, his father told him that since that time, every male in our family has been blind, where the female children have been sighted—although every generation has had a Theophane. The translation of which is, "One Who Speaks with God." Originally, this book was printed in Greek, and every Theophane has used it. The cover contains the DNA signature, in the form of hand and finger oil, from everyone who has touched it. You will learn more about this if you decide to begin your training.

Like my male relatives before me, I am able to see clearly into the minds and hearts of those I have been assigned to meet. Because you have been given this book, you have passed our first test; and there are more. Many, for a variety of reasons, do not complete the training. Your problems, suffering, and worries have provided the raw material for your transformation. Your kindness, compassion, and instruction will create the alchemy necessary for your graduation to the next level.

Just as there have been many Theophanes, there have also been many teachers. You are not obligated to contact the teacher identified on your card. In fact, do not make contact unless you sincerely desire to know the real reasons for your earthly concerns, as well as their solutions. The price you will pay for your knowledge will be that you must give up all your excuses and become who you really are, with no pretending. As a result of your training, you will want to spend the rest of your life serving others, and in so doing you will find joy and satisfaction in living, as well as all of the answers you seek.

Do not contact your teacher unless you have decided to walk past your fear and step into the unknown. I promise that your journey will be fulfilling beyond your dreams. The choice is yours.

Blessings,

Theophane

I needed a nap. How could these few pages make me so tired? I decided to get a coffee refill. Since I had been alone in the back section, I decided to leave the book on the table.

When I returned, the book was gone. Panic! I felt like I had misplaced the wedding rings and the priest had just asked for them. *What do I do? Think! Panic does not work!* But the fight for rationality was overwhelming. *Breathe! Sit down and breathe.* I did and noticed a door that I suspected led to the kitchen.

When I opened the door, I saw the cook tracing the fleur-de-lis with his right index finger as the book rested on his work counter. His left hand was busy turning eggs. He looked Asian.

"That's my book. You took it!" My tone was accusatory and angry.

He responded loudly in what sounded like Chinese and with his left hand put down the spatula and picked up a meat cleaver. His tone and gesture strongly suggested that I should get out of his kitchen. As I backed up, I bowed to him. I remembered the old Charlie Chan movies and how he was always bowing to everyone, even his enemies. I'd try it, and when I did, he put down the persuader.

Magically, it was like I had turned on a switch. He smiled, bowed back, and looked at me quizzically.

I touched my chest with the index finger of my right hand and then, put my two hands together, as if they were holding a book. I pointed to the book and said, "My book!"

"You book? Ah! You book! Berry sorry," and he handed it back to me.

Theophane was right, it had become a treasure; though I had no idea what the treasure would cost.

Chapter Two

Being banished to some isolated, cloud-covered island is probably less painful than.

The Summer of the Great Silence

The series of events and coincidences that led to meeting Theophane made me think about the adage that says: "when the student is ready, the teacher appears." It sounds like a message from a fortune cookie, but I believe it.

Before my meeting on the train platform, I had come to a point in my life where I questioned and doubted that anything good could happen to me. If there was a phone number I could have called and said, "I give up and I don't care," followed by a van that showed up at my door to take me away, I would have made the call. I guess we've all been there, some of us more frequently than others, and I suspect anyone who has children has been there many times.

But there was more. I was tired, bone tired. Too much work and not enough play. I had nothing left in my emotional, spiritual, or physical gas tanks.

My divorce was finalized and my children were very angry with me. I've come to realize that most sons and daughters, even when they are adults, want Mom and Dad together—regardless of the quality of their marriage. My former wife was, and is, a good person and a great mother. Unfortunately, we came from very different places and, in time, we did not meet each other's expectations. That was it. We each had expectations and they were different.

I could not expect my daughters to understand, and at the time, neither of them was speaking to me. Being banished to some isolated, cloud-covered island is probably less painful than seeing your kids walk the other way when they see you.

From June until the end of August, I worked on publishing articles to support my case for tenure at the university where I taught. I had retired from being an administrator for a mid-sized city and had worked for five years as a university professor. I had moved to the Jersey Shore and spent most of my free time riding my bicycle and walking on the beach.

That summer I recall thinking: *maybe I'm being prepared to become a hermit. Maybe I'll end up living in a cave on some Greek island inhabited only by goats.*

There were no visits from friends or family. I felt as if I had dropped off the face of the Earth and nobody cared. My only phone calls were from my mother. I think of mothers as the Last Chance Hotel. If your mom doesn't call, either she has some major issues or you are one lousy son or daughter. Moms are usually the last to abandon ship. The whole world could be chasing you down like a rabid coyote and Mom would hide you in the cellar. Most moms are very special people. Mine fits into that category. Without her phone calls, maybe I would have jumped on a freighter, and while on the way to China been lost at sea in a typhoon instead of writing this story. See how quickly my imagination jumps into overdrive.

There were other extremely upsetting family issues. Some laundry should not be hung out on the line, and so, to protect the guilty as well as the innocent, these challenges will remain confidential.

By the fall, the isolation had taken its toll and a part of me felt dead. I had lost my joy. I like to sing and that summer, I just couldn't. I named it The Summer of the Great Silence.

During one of my bike rides, I remember asking myself why I didn't have more money. Even before our divorce, there were always money problems. I consoled myself with the recognition that lots of folks with and without kids have to struggle.

How come it seems that everybody I know has more money than I do? What did I do wrong? I don't smoke. The only time I drink beer is when I have spaghetti and meatballs. Maybe instead of eating lunch at the local diner, I should have been brown bagging it for the past twenty-five years. By not spending eight dollars a day for lunch and the tip five days a week, fifty working weeks a year, in a year, I would have saved two thousand dollars. If I invested the money wisely, maybe I could have doubled or tripled my money. What if I bought Microsoft early? Maybe I'd own a small country somewhere, instead of smiling at people I don't like so I wouldn't lose my job. My thoughts were sounding like a Jackie Mason routine.

It wasn't just the money, the divorce, the work concerns, and the kids not talking to me—it was me. Everything I had worked for was gone, and I was unsure if I would be able to keep my job unless I successfully published. I felt alone, tired, financially challenged, and most of all, pissed off. I know there are more refined ways to express my discontent, but pissed off says it like it was.

About a year before I met Theophane, I'd finished a book that I was counting on to pull me out of emotional and financial debt. Writing, for as long as I can remember, had helped me create order from disorder. It's given me a sense of control when I feel I don't have any. I was hoping that the book would help me find my way out of what had become a severe case of feeling sorry for myself. Too often, I had heard myself whining, and I really dislike whining.

The coincidences that had brought Theophane to me had their roots at a Mystery Writers of America Meeting near Gramercy Park in Manhattan. Though the book I'd completed was in the self-help genre, I knew that publishing agents for all genres would be there, and my colleague, Mary Ellen, a published author, knew some of them.

The guest speaker was an FBI agent who specialized in profiling serial killers. Mary Ellen knew that I'd finished my book, *Anxiety Relief without Medication,* and while her agent Mel was speaking to the profiler before dinner, she interrupted them by walking over and kissing Mel on the lips. I remember thinking, *that kiss could burn the paint off a bridge.* He seemed to forget whatever it was they were talking about and he introduced her to the speaker.

I had stepped aside to survey the kiss from the most advantageous perspective, and when she motioned to me, I stepped forward.

"Mel, meet Andy. Andy, Mel is my agent and you two will like each other. Mel, Andy's a genius and he needs an agent. He's just finished a self-help book."

Genius? She has to be kidding! I'm on the slippery slope to nowhere … genius? But her endorsement was appreciated.

She turned, took the profiler's arm, and walked him toward the bar. Mel and I watched as, arm in arm, she navigated.

Mel said, "You've just witnessed a demonstration of Mary Ellen's power. It's kryptonite. Male editors, publishers, and in this case, FBI agents, have no antidote for it. Let's have a drink."

And we did.

"So, what's your book about?"

I explained that most psychiatrists prescribe medications for their patients with intense anxiety, and they generally don't give them tools they can use to cope with the source of these feelings. So, unless they learn the cause of their anxiety and how to healthfully address it, folks really don't get better; they just take a pill that masks their symptoms. In time, when their body acclimates to the dosage, they have to take more to get the same effect. It's a pharmaceutical golden goose.

"What's your answer? What will the reader learn?"

"Do you want me to condense the fifteen chapters into a sound bite?"

"That would be nice," he responded.

"Most folks live in the past or the future. People who live in the past beat themselves up emotionally because of things that happened or things they've done that they are unhappy about. They can't let go, and the record of their failures keeps playing in their mind, over and over. They can't turn it off and they can't change what happened. Others live in the future. They worry that there won't be enough money, love, recognition, or job security. They're scared rabbits. People who live in the present and work toward doing what they can to be happy and successful on a day-by-day basis do much better with anxiety."

"That's it? Learn to live in the present and you're healed?"

"Remember, I'm trying for a sound bite. It's the learning to live in the present, and not the past or the future that the book's about. It's not an original idea. Others have done it. Spenser Johnson's book, *The Precious Present*, had some great suggestions for living a fulfilling life—my book is very different. It's more of a how-to manual. I give people the information they need to understand their anxiety and use it to enhance their day-to-day living. The knowledge takes away the fear."

"I think I'm a candidate for your book," Mel said. I've walked around with a knot in my stomach for so long, I wouldn't know how it feels without it. The evidence is in my medicine cabinet; I'm interested."

The shoemaker's children have no shoes and the psychologist who wrote a book about living in the present is living in the past and the future. I felt phony.

He gave me his card and said, "Call my secretary; she'll set something up. I'll need to see some chapters. Bring them with you."

Mel patted and brushed his hair and, after he was satisfied with the unseen result, waived at a young lady wearing a black, dangerously low-cut dress at the end of the bar. She smiled and off he swaggered, like some modern pirate on his way to a booty call. Our meeting was over. There was no, "I'm looking forward to meeting with you," or "make sure you call."

I stood there and thought about the process that had unfolded: Mary Ellen, the kiss, the arm-in-arm walk, and my talk with Mel. I decided to refill my drink and wait for Mary Ellen to return—she didn't.

Chapter Three

*I could have sworn Rudyard
was talking to me.*

The Sign

The train ride. The scarecrow. The book. The Chinese cook. The legend of Tiresias. The names on the back page. Who was the Gifted One? Why me? What tests would I have to pass? Was this all a joke? A con? Or was this the chance of a lifetime?

There were too many unanswered questions, and I needed time to think. A blind man in a worn-out coat who told me I had passed the first test because I gave him a handout had trumped the meeting with Mel.

I ordered a third cup of coffee before I phoned Sandra and told her I wouldn't be able to make the meeting. I wasn't feeling well, I explained, and would like to reschedule. It was a half lie. The truth was that I wasn't in the mood to participate in the publishing dance with Mel. I just couldn't do it.

"I hope you feel better," she responded in a tone that sounded like she meant it.

What do I do now? It was my call. The ball was in my court and I had no idea what I was going to do with it.

Okay! Think. Be rational. I decided to try the Ben Franklin method.

Take a sheet of paper and divide it in half. On one side, put all the reasons I should call the number on the card and on the other, all the reasons I shouldn't. Rational. Logical. Systematic. I was proud of myself. I took out a piece of paper and began—pro on one side and con on the other. It wasn't working. No, I didn't want to be logical. A blind messenger with an ancient book wasn't about logic. I needed a sign—something that would provide guidance.

A week went by and no sign. There is a voice I have in my head that guides me. I believe we all have one, if we are quiet enough and listen. Since my meeting with Theophane, the voice had whispered countless times: "Let it go. It's crazy! Get on with your life!"

Another few days went by and I was in my doctor's office, waiting for my three-month blood pressure check, still looking for a sign. As usual, he was late, and after deciding I was not interested in reading *Ladies Home Journal* or *Better Homes and Gardens,* the only magazines there, I decided to read the framed journal articles on the wall. He had written them and was showing off.

He also had framed his degrees, as well as a copy of Kipling's poem, *If.* The poem is a father's message to his son about what it means to be a man. At about the middle, I felt goose bumps on my arms. I could have sworn Rudyard was talking to me. It read:

> If you can make one heap of all your winnings
> And risk it on one turn of pitch-and-toss,
> And lose, and start again at your beginnings
> And never breathe a word about your loss;
> If you can force your heart and nerve and sinew
> To serve your turn long after they are gone,
> And so hold on when there is nothing in you
> Except the Will which says to them: 'Hold on!'
> If you can talk with crowds and keep your virtue,
> 'Or walk with Kings - nor lose the common touch,
> If neither foes nor loving friends can hurt you,
> If all men count with you, but none too much;
> If you can fill the unforgiving minute

With sixty seconds' worth of distance run,
Yours is the Earth and everything that's in it,
And - which is more - you'll be a Man, my son!

That was it. The sign I needed. Take a chance. Go for it. I had kept the card in my front right-hand pants pocket. I touched it and knew I'd be making the call.

The area code was in Arizona. The woman at the other end of the phone line had not identified herself, but answered the phone by saying, "We are pleased you called, Andy!" *How did she know who it was? I was calling from a public phone. Maybe it was because I was calling from New Jersey? No need to get overly mystical.*

She asked me to write down the directions. When she finished, she asked me to repeat them. After I did, she said, "The man you are going to meet is recognized by many as the world's greatest healer. There are folks who believe he is a myth—I promise you he is real. There are powerful politicians, fabulously rich men and women, as well as many people of national and international importance who want to meet him. To meet him, you must be chosen. He does not care about status, money, or power; he is interested in what is in your heart and what you are willing to do for others."

There was no discussion about whether I should bring warm clothes, a hat, or sunscreen. Her voice was bubbly, the voice of someone who gets excited about the little things like playing with a puppy, writing a letter to a friend, or watching a sunset. I wanted to meet her, and I reminded myself that the voice doesn't always match the person. She could look like a lady wrestler and chew tobacco. I was about to ask her name when her voice changed. It became firm, no-nonsense; it was the voice of a judge who was sentencing an unrepentant criminal.

"You are expected to arrive at 4:30 AM, and lateness will not be tolerated for any reason." She didn't say what would occur if I happened to be late, and I didn't want to know. Her message was clear.

As if a switch were thrown, the bubbles were back in her voice and before she hung up said, "I'm looking forward to meeting you, Andy."

I still didn't know her name, and she didn't give me time to ask. There was no pause in her conversation that would provide an opening. I felt nervous. The feeling was reminiscent of the one I used to get before I returned kickoffs for my high school football team. It took me a few seconds to hang up the phone. I stood there looking at the phone—*a new piece of the puzzle.*

Spring break was about to start, and as a college professor I had ten days off. I had read and reread Theophane's three-page book more than a dozen times. The cover had a distinctive spicy smell that lingered in my nostrils. The book had become my treasure and I had no idea if it was also my ticket to enter into a world that would open doors I didn't know existed.

Chapter Four

The smell of the desert could have been a thousand or maybe a million years old.

Alone at Night in the Desert

When I boarded the Continental flight from Newark to Phoenix, I felt like a kid going to camp. What would happen? Who would I meet? Would the trip change my life or did someone get my name from the Kripalu mailing list and figure I'd be a sucker for a mystical con scheme? I ordered a gin and tonic and put Theophanes's book on my lap. I didn't trust placing it in the luggage. *Maybe a drink will take the edge off?*

I tried to sleep, but my mind kept running and rewinding the meeting with Theophane; reading the book in the café, finding the poem, and my phone conference with the mystery woman. The replays failed to provide anything new.

Maybe I needed a second gin and tonic. I wasn't the pilot. I didn't have to drive home. I reminded myself that the second one never tasted as good as the first. I felt the warmth of the first drink on its journey to my stomach. An hour later, the second one verified my thoughts about the effects of first and second drinks. After the second drink, I closed my eyes and tried to sleep. An hour and a half later, I snored so loudly I woke myself up. I realized my head was leaning on the shoulder of the woman next to me. I looked at her and said, "Sorry!"

She glared at me in return and looked out the window. She had been working on a Sudoku puzzle, and I suspect my snoring and posture had interfered with her concentration. She was a large-framed, stern-looking woman, and I believed she'd probably make a good prison guard. Even the most hardened criminals wouldn't dare ask her for a cigarette. I hoped the woman on the phone didn't look like her.

I had the directions to where I was going on a small notepad in the breast pocket of my jacket. I touched it to make sure it was still there. When I did, it made me think of the book I had placed on my lap. It wasn't there. I panicked. *Not again. The last time this happened, I had to rely on memories of Charlie Chan to get me through.* I could feel my pulse quicken and my heart race. I looked toward my feet and noticed that the book had fallen on the floor in front of Ms. Congeniality. I had two choices: ask her to pick it up or go for it myself and risk placing my arm in a position very close to her crotch. I decided to ask for her assistance.

She glared again. She attempted to reach the book, but she couldn't make it.

"No problem," I said. "I'll get it when we're deplaning."

"Whad you mean deplanink?"

Her accent was Eastern European and I mused that she was probably on her way to a world-class powerlifting contest.

"When we are leaving the plane."

Her facial expression made my think she would like me to leave now at thirty thousand feet.

"Oh! Ven ve leaf."

I smiled and she went back to the puzzle.

We arrived at 5:17 PM, and when I stepped into the aisle to let her pass, so I could get the book, she nodded and said, "Nice talkink to you."

I couldn't resist. As I moved toward the book, I answered, "It was fun."

At about 6:30 PM, I arrived at the Avis counter and they had the car ready. I wanted something with four-wheel drive and decided on a dark blue Nissan Pathfinder.

I needed to eat. I couldn't eat the lunch on the plane. I had no appetite. Now I was hungry.

Wanting to get away from the airport and the crowds, I drove for about an hour and found a Black Bear restaurant. They're a chain, like Bennigan's in the Northeast. It had a Western ambiance and was a place truckers on a long haul would look forward to. I ordered a cheeseburger, fries, and coffee, and by the second cup, I was ready to review the directions and transpose them to a map. By my calculations, his home seemed to be in the middle of the desert. There was nothing around it for thirty miles.

When I finished at the Black Bear, I checked my watch and it was 8:19 PM. I was bone tired, despite my siesta on the plane, and needed a nap. I figured my trip would take three hours, maybe three and a half. If I left at 10:00, I'd have plenty of time in case I got lost. I pulled the Pathfinder around the back of the restaurant, pushed the seat back, locked the doors, and tried to sleep. I had the book and directions on the seat next to me.

I awoke with a start when a policeman knocked on my window. When I opened my eyes, he said, "Are you okay, sir?"

My immediate concern was, *where am I?*

"Fine, officer. I just needed a little nap."

He smiled and said, "Drive safely, sir."

What time was it? It was too dark to see my watch, so I turned on the cabin light and saw that it was 11:17 PM.

I had slept for almost three hours. *Was that possible?* I needed to use the bathroom, but didn't want to. I was concerned about the time. I'd have to drive faster. I could hear her voice: "no excuses" and "4:30

AM." I felt like I was sixteen and on probation for lateness—one more infraction and no prom.

I made the pit stop in record time and was on my way. It was 11:27.

After about an hour, the hum of the air conditioner and the sound of the tires on the road were inviting me to close my eyes. *I shouldn't be tired. I just had a great nap. How can I be tired?* I turned the air conditioner off and opened the windows. *Maybe that would help?*

It didn't.

I turned on the radio and listened to a talk show about global warming and the pollution of our planet. The guest was a Greek scientist who spoke about the destruction of forests around the world and especially the damage that continues in South America to the rainforest. His message was that the forests of the world take in carbon dioxide and create oxygen. Fewer trees mean more carbon dioxide and an increase in global warming.

Another nail in our coffin; I wonder how long we have before the coastal cities are underwater? And, nobody seems to be doing a damn thing about it?

I turned the radio off. Too depressing. I sucked in a deep breath of desert air. The night desert has a very distinctive smell. It's an earthy, sensual aroma. Primitive. Timeless. It could be a thousand or maybe a million years old. I liked it.

Her voice kept me going. "Lateness will not be tolerated for any reason."

I followed the directions with the odometer, 17.3 miles; make a left, 22.9 miles a right, etc. I was sweating but decided, *so far, so good.* The directions matched perfectly. It was 2:19 AM and there was no house in sight. I was getting sleepy again. By my calculations, I had about another forty-five minutes to go.

Was I the moth flying into the flame?

I found his home about an hour and a half later, although I did get lost. I had passed it because it couldn't be seen from the roadway.

There was a steep berm on both sides of the road, which rose about ten feet, and the house was hidden behind it. It was in a depression about a hundred feet from the side of the road. I estimated that the roof of the house was about five feet lower than the roadway.

I found the driveway, stopped the car, pushed my seat back, and waited. The house seemed small—maybe six rooms. It was hard to tell in the dark. *Who is this guy who is supposed to be the world's greatest healer? What's going to happen to me?* It was 3:50 AM and my bladder was screaming for relief. While attempting to cope with my need for a pit stop, I heard a noise from the house. *Suppose someone came out. I couldn't risk it. I'd have to suppress the urge and wait until I was in the house.*

It was 4:27 when I walked toward the door. I couldn't find a doorbell. There was a knocker on the door the same shape as the fleur-de-lis on the card. I waited about thirty seconds and knocked. There was no response, and I couldn't see any lights.

As I stood there in the darkness, I traced the edges of the knocker with my right index finger. It felt cold and smooth. I knocked again, but louder. I could feel my heart pounding. *The sound of the metal on metal could wake the dead. If somebody doesn't open the door soon, I'm going to water the shrubs.* In my imagination, that picture was processing like a developing Polaroid.

There I am watering the flowers of the Shell Answer Man of metaphysics and he answers the door and catches me. I say, "Oh gee! I'm awfully sorry. It's just that I couldn't hold it any longer."

And he would say, "I knew anyone from New Jersey would be a mistake." My fantasy continues and he sends me home, much to the embarrassment of myself and fellow New Jerseyans who will read about it the following Sunday in the *Star Ledger*.

No answer. I waited, and the nervous feeling came back. Then I heard movement. Someone or something was coming. I wondered if I was on my way to being kidnapped, beaten, tortured, murdered, or all of the above.

Chapter Five

*If he rises up from his seat on the carpet
and levitates, I'm out of here.*

Kemosabe

The sounds became footsteps. I took a deep breath and waited. I could feel the sweat on my hands. The door opened. The fatigue was gone, and I felt my heart pounding in my throat. I was ready (or at least I believed I was ready) to speak to a man I was led to believe is the greatest healer in the world.

I saw his worn cowboy boots first. Then the faded dungarees, and the silver belt buckle with a representation of planet Earth in the palm of a bear paw —and seven stars around the perimeter. It was stunning!

He wore a short-sleeved red-and-white plaid lumberjack shirt that reminded me of a barroom tablecloth.

His shoulders looked like he was wearing quarterback shoulder pads, the condensed version that allow for more freedom of motion. His chest and shoulders were much bigger than his waist. *This guy looks like some kind of athlete.* I still hadn't looked at his face.

The moment of truth had arrived. I was going to look the legend in the eye, and he was going to size me up, and I would do the same with him. Before I could look up, he extended his hand. I shook it as I looked toward his eyes. Damn! He was wearing sunglasses. Sky-blue mirrored lenses with silver wire frames and a crew cut. The Gifted One looked like a hybrid between a lumberjack and a racecar driver. *Jesus! I hadn't expected this. I had figured a white robe, sandals, and hair down to his rear end. Maybe I'm at the wrong ranch?*

"Hi, Kemosabe," he said as we shook hands. He then led me down a dimly lit hallway. Softly, a recording of Willie Nelson singing *Stardust* played. Halfway down the hall, we turned right and entered a white stucco room with a stone fireplace on the southern wall. I asked to use the restroom, and he pointed the way.

I returned and looked around; no desk, tables, or chairs, in a room that was flanked by a floor-to-ceiling perimeter of bookshelves. Books, journals, and manuscripts were shelved, some neatly and some on top of each other. Hand-carved wooden identification plaques sat on top of the bookshelves. On the north wall it read Religion, Art, and Music. The sign on the south wall, which included above and around the fireplace read, Politics, Economics, and Science. The west wall bookshelves were identified as, Social Science, Self-help, Healing, and Psychology, and the east wall bookshelves, Health and Education.

The rug on the polished hardwood floor looked like Southwest American Indian and smelled of sage. On the brick ledge next to the fireplace, logs were neatly piled like rows of ammunition on a battleship. The rug was worn where two—as the Irish would pronounce "arses"—had sat, as their owners faced the fireplace. He invited me to add to the wear of the space about three feet to the right of his. I remember thinking: *Good Lord, he certainly doesn't spend his money on furniture.*

I identified the sandalwood scent from the candle that burned in front of the empty fireplace. My awareness darted from the source of the fragrance back to his initial greeting, Kemosabe. I hadn't heard that name since I was a boy. It was Tonto's name for the Lone Ranger. Supposedly, it meant friend in an undefined American Indian dialect.

It could just as easily have meant knucklehead and none of us ten-year-olds would have known the difference.

We sat down and watched the candle flame flicker. *Atavistic—no doubt about it. We've been staring for millions of years, and only in the last fifty had TV replaced the flame. There must be something very human about staring. Maybe there's a human need to stare. Before fire, we stared at the stars, after fire, TV, and now the computer.*

How many people watch tropical fish? The fish don't do anything special. They swim. That's it—and yet we stare. We stare at fish being themselves and say, "Wow! Look at those fish!" as if they were doing something unexpected.

I smelled the cactus before I saw them. On both sides of the fireplace stood miniature barrel cacti about two feet tall. The cactus motif was continued throughout the room in so unobtrusive a manner that initially I hadn't noticed them. There were all sorts of cacti, including some I'd never seen before. From my seat, I began to feel as if I was a cowboy sitting in front of a mini desert campfire waiting for the other cowboys to come in from the range. I was still musing about the cowboy setting when he said, "It is not a coincidence that Theophane met you at the station. I have been looking for candidates to meet with me to change the world. It needs to be healed, you know."

Whoa! I was here to lose weight, get healthy, improve my family relationships, and maybe find another job. Changing the world didn't fit into my plans for the week. He still had the sunglasses on, and I was wondering if he was blind when he said, "My eyes were injured by a bomb blast when I was a little boy. They are very sensitive to light. That is why I wear the sunglasses."

Interesting! I was mentally asking myself about his glasses and he answered the question I was thinking.

He continued, "You are here because you know your life is less than it could be and you want to be happy and healthy. Currently, someone or something is keeping you from realizing your human potential. By the way, that someone may be you. It is sometimes that simple."

I wanted to hear more.

He paused and said, "You may be unhappy and unhealthy because you insist on controlling things you have no control over. You have been disappointed and feel that fate has not been kind to you. People and life, in your mind, have let you down, and your dreams have not come true. Your life is not the way you believe it is supposed to be. In your mind, you have a projection of how your life should look, and your reality is not in agreement with it. How am I doing, Kemosabe?"

"You're on target," I answered, followed by, "Am I supposed to call you Tonto?"

He smiled and breathed a sound that I suspected that was a laugh.

"I like the sound of the word ... Kemosabe ... and what I liked even more was the respect in Tonto's voice when he used it. Whenever I meet someone with whom I want to develop a relationship for the first time, I use the term Kemosabe. For me, it means respected friend. It is the first step toward making that person my respected friend. Intention is very important, you know."

Once again, I was thinking about his choice of the word Kemosabe, when he began to speak about the thought that was processing in my mind. *Strange!*

"As we work together during the next week, you will find that I provide you with no direct answers to your questions or concerns. This may seem unusual to you; although I have learned that even though they say they do, people really do not want answers. I know this because when I was young, I gave answers. I told those who came to me what they needed to know to fix their problems. It did not work. Instead, many of them never came back, and sometimes they told their friends or family that my name was quite inappropriate. That instead of the Gifted One, a more accurate title might be the Inadequate One or maybe, the Dim One."

He followed up his response with another loud, "Hah," and his smile told me that he thought what he said was amusing.

"What I learned is that when you give someone an answer and they do not have to work for it, they do not own it."

Again he made that "Hah!" sound and continued. "They have not worked it through and paid their dues. It is too easy. Like the parent who tells a child not do something because they know it will produce a result the child does want and the child does it anyway. The child did not want an answer, even if he or she said they did. They needed the experience of learning the outcome of their actions. Life is about the experience, not the answers."

He continued, "I hear you met Theophane. He is one of our best. He has a talent for it. He knows."

Knows what? I wondered.

"He knew you were ready. He knew you wanted desperately to change but you did not know how. He knew you needed a coach— someone who would bring you along at your own pace, someone who would open your eyes and awaken you to the possibilities of your life, which right now are far beyond your ability to realize. He knew you needed me, and I am glad you are here, because I need you."

Why does he need me?

He was answering the questions I wondered but didn't ask. He had done it now a number of times. This was spooky. *If he rises up from his seat on the carpet and levitates, I'm out of here. I'm bolting for the door, jumping in the car, and getting myself out of the Twilight Zone.*

When I was through thinking, he put his hand on my shoulder and said, "Do not worry. I never levitate during the first lesson."

We both laughed, an infectious laugh that dismissed some of my anxiety. He was goofing on himself, goofing on me, and at the same time, trying to put me at ease. Not an easy task!

We had been together for only a few minutes and already I felt a level of comfort that was unusual for me. I wasn't sure if it was something in his manner of speech or the tone of his voice. There was something about him that made me feel safe, despite the fact that I was sitting with a man I didn't know, on a worn American Indian rug, at a remote desert ranch, in the middle of the night, staring at a candle. A man introduced to me as a result of an encounter with a blind human scarecrow on a subway platform in New York.

I couldn't help but think of how I would explain it to the police if this whole experience was the initial stage of some bizarre cult induction that would leave me wandering naked and penniless in the desert.

"You see, officer, I was on a subway platform at Thirty-third Street in Manhattan when I met this unusual-looking man who asked me for a handout. I gave him enough money to buy lunch, and in return he gave me a card and a book and said they were what I really needed. In the middle of the card it read The Gifted One, and at the bottom of the card there was a phone number. I called the number, got an appointment, took a plane to Arizona, and drove to his ranch, arriving before dawn. From what you're telling me, it's now four months later and the last thing I remember was sitting on a rug in front of a lit candle and talking to him."

Even Columbo wouldn't want to be involved. I could almost hear Peter Falk saying in his humble, apologetic voice, "Sir, what we have here is a problem. It seems to me that this may be a very complex problem so, sir, if you'll just give me a moment." After he paces back and forth a few times and takes the cigar out of his mouth, he turns to me and says, "Sir, I hope you're not offended by my question but ... do you take any medication?"

Now that I had created a worst—or near-worst—case scenario, I adjusted the frame of my glasses so they sat higher on the bridge of my nose. It's a nervous habit, and I do it unconsciously when I'm trying to figure something out. Sometimes I attempt to perform the ritual in the shower and realize that I'm not wearing glasses. It's like a pre-thinking ritual, and after I did it, I asked myself: *how does this feel? Do you think Theophane and the Gifted One are homicidal maniacs? If you do, get out before he brings the Kool-Aid. If you don't, relax and go with it. It's too late and too far away to get a room, so when you go to your room, wedge a chair under the doorknob and find something to fight with: a lamp, a chair, or maybe a heavy ashtray in a sock.*

After my thoughts of self-defense, the Gifted One said matter-of-factly, "You are having a difficult time relaxing."

"Yes! This is a little overwhelming."

"To be cautious is prudent," he said. "Being cautious is part of the natural selection process. Those who are not cautious in the presence of potential danger perished. If you were not a little concerned, it would be very unusual. Everyone who comes here will be worried about what is going to happen. They are uncertain of what our meeting will bring to their lives. Soon, you will tell yourself that there is no need to be fearful."

He paused for a few seconds and continued, "As the days unfold, you will have your answers without me telling you. You are here to learn some important, yet very simple, life concepts, and you will also receive twelve gifts. The gifts will open doors to help you to change your life; and for them to be effective they require daily practice. When it is time to leave, I promise you will be in one piece and have a renewed sense of purpose and the knowledge you need to make the world a better place. In essence, I am preparing you to do your life's work, which includes assisting me in healing the world."

He paused again, "Think of me as your coach. In fact, please do not call me The Gifted One. The people who gave me the name were very well meaning, and I was, and remain, flattered; but it makes me think of a porn star. Call me Coach. Everybody who comes here calls me Coach. Names that do not capture the essence of who a person is—do not mean anything to me. Once you are tested, I will give you an Indian name that describes your spirit. I have some ideas already but ... not yet. I need more time. We need to talk more. There will be plenty of time. For now, I will call you Joe. Until I give the male initiates their Indian name, I call them Joe. If the trainee is a woman, I call her Lucy. I like that name. I remember it from the TV show, *I*

Love Lucy. When I was a young monk, we were not allowed to watch television. When I was about eleven and on the way to a monastery in Hawaii, we visited for a few days with a local family and the children were watching *I Love Lucy.* She had done something foolish and Ricky, her husband, was annoyed. He came into the room and said, in his Cuban accent, 'Lucy, you have some 'splaining to do!' Her eyes opened wide and she made a worried face as she told him a silly story to cover her actions. It was a funny show. Lucy was the first American woman I remember as a child.

"Some men do not like it when I call them Joe and some women do not like Lucy. I ask them, 'what does a name mean?' It is not our name that is important; it is what we do. When we die, we will be remembered for what we have done and who we were. We do not need a name for that. People remember our spirit. They remember who we were and how we interacted with them. The Indian name I give you will tell far more about your spirit than your real name. One of my favorite activities is capturing one's spirit in their Indian name. It is great fun … getting it just right. There is much to be said for simple pleasures."

At that point, I still had lots of questions about him. Where did he come from? What exactly would we be doing? Why was I chosen to meet him? Even though I didn't know him, he spoke to me as if we were close friends and that we shared a tacit understanding about my safety; that I did not have to worry; that I would be okay. I hoped my intuition was on target.

"Joe, you are here because life has provided you with the raw material for some major progress. You have come to question parts of your life that, for a long time, remained unexamined. Your uncertainty will assist me in helping you open your eyes, and I will guide you to see things you have never seen before—though you may have looked at them many times. No one changes unless they have enough pain, and the anxiety of your uncertainty is your passport to change. I will guide you, and should you decide to do so, you will guide many."

His English pronunciation was flawless. He did have a faint accent that could have been Asian, though I couldn't begin to guess the country. I had become Joe and not Kemosabe. I was too tired to ask questions. I told him I appreciated his invitation. He nodded, and I remember thinking that a clean bed would make me very happy when he said, "You will be awakened at 8:00 AM, and we will meet in this room at 8:30. All of your unanswered questions will be addressed during your stay." My watch read 5:01.

He led me to my room. The bed was covered with a rust-brown blanket with yellow, green, and blue American Indian designs that were simple and elegant. The blanket was probably Navajo.

The chest of drawers and matching nightstand had been freshly painted to match the yellow in the blanket. The green ceramic cowboy-boot lamp on the nightstand looked like it belonged in a child's room. The walls were daisy yellow. I found no television, radio, or clock. When I wondered how I would know when it was time to get up he said, "Just rest; I will make sure you get up on time."

The desk and chair matched the rust brown in the blanket, and the glow from the fluorescent desk lamp in the shape of long horns reminded me of a Kincaid painting. I showered and fell into bed. The next thing I heard was the tinkling of three high-pitched bells. I had attended a monastery retreat in my twenties, and there I had heard temple bells. That's what these sounded like.

I wasn't dreaming when I watched the door creak open. I had overlooked wedging a chair back under the handle. *This is it; this is the part where I am going to be killed in my sleep and sacrificed to atone for someone's sin.* I held my breath and watched.

Chapter Six

We have come together to create a harmony you will take with you and you will teach others to create their harmony.

The Awakening

I waited anxiously, and after the door opened, watched in relief as a cup of steaming hot tea was delivered to the table next to the door by an arm that was tanned, delicate, and obviously female. No words were spoken, and after the tea was placed on the table, the door was closed. I could feel my heart thumping in my chest, and I suspected the same mystery woman who had spoken to me on the phone delivered the tea.

After I brushed my teeth, I indulged in a quick wash and change of clothes, and I headed toward the library. When I got there, Coach was already seated with his legs crossed in front of him facing the fireplace. The smoke from one stick of incense was enough to fill the air with the scent of sage. Two white, eight-inch candles set in thick bronze holders stood guard in front of the sand-filled vase that held the burning sage.

When I entered, he asked me to sit down and close my eyes.

"Breathe, Joe! Inhale the sage and let it enter every cell in your body. Inhale slowly. Exhale slowly. Give thanks for the breath that sustains you and the sage that is purifying you."

"To whom do I give thanks?"

He didn't answer.

Before I closed my eyes, I saw him take out a small animal-skin pouch and pour what looked like cornmeal into his hand. He sprinkled it in the vase that held the incense.

We sat there and breathed for what seemed like five or ten minutes, but it could have been fifteen or twenty.

I was thinking that time didn't seem to matter when I heard him say, "You may open your eyes. Let us begin."

"Everything we do here is for a reason," he explained. "It may not seem like it, but as you will come to see, everything has a purpose that will be of assistance as you progress through your awakening. I say awakening because, though you do not know it, in many ways, you are asleep. It is very human of you to not be fully awake; that is part of the reason you are here. To help you open your eyes and ears."

He took a deep breath, waited about two seconds, and said, "When Theophane met you, you were on your way to a publisher and you were very stressed. You were worried. Do you know what you were worried about?"

"Yes, I was worried he wouldn't like the book or he wouldn't market it properly. I was worried he wouldn't pay me what I felt the book was worth. I was worried about a lot of things. I was worried about my kids. They're having problems getting their lives in order, and one of them is still trying to heal from an ugly divorce, not that any divorce is pretty.

"I think what worries me most is the thought of my oldest daughter getting sick, because she's taken on a second job in order to pay the bills. In her teens, when she was under a lot of stress, she had a seizure. It scared me.

"When I met Theophane, I was worried about my health. In the last few years, I became hypertensive. I had injured my knee and walked with a limp for months. I started a new job as a university professor, and I was concerned about getting tenured. There were always money problems. There was always a shortage of cash.

"So, what was I stressed about? The book, the kids, the job, my health, and of course, money. It's probably the major concern most of us have: will there be enough money?"

"Look at the candle, what do you see?"

"A flame," I answered.

"What else?"

"The candles, the candle holders, the vase, the incense stick, and the fireplace bricks."

"Is that all?" he asked.

"Yes ... I think so. Should there be anything else?"

"Do you see light?"

"Yes, of course," I responded.

"Do you see darkness?"

"Yes."

"But you did not see the darkness right away. You saw a flame; you saw a candle; you saw incense and bricks, and yet, because it was obvious, you did not see the darkness. Hah!" He laughed and smiled at me. I felt like the mouse—and the cat was enjoying himself.

"Very amusing, yes?"

I nodded a perfunctory nod; although I had not found the exercise as riotous as he did. *I hope it gets better than this.* I feel like I'm watching young Caine interacting with Master Po at the Shaolin monastery on the '70s TV show *Kung Fu.*

"Is your goal in life to be the best self you can be?"

"Yes," I responded.

"Is your desire to find the path that will lead you to that goal?"

"Yes."

"And now you can see how the path can be right in front of you and you cannot see it because it is so obvious. There are signs, which, for a variety of reasons, people choose to ignore. Worry, poor health, problems sleeping or eating, depression, unhappiness, lack of energy, feeling unfulfilled … these are signs. They mean something. Often, they mean the man or woman experiencing them has impotent goals, goals that are not exciting, challenging, or meaningful. Later, we will talk more about understanding the need for potent goals."

I wanted to know more right away, but I sensed it wasn't going to happen.

"You have been chosen to come here because you have not been able to find your path. You want to make your life count for something, but you do not know how. That is our purpose, to help you find your path so you can help other people find theirs. But first, you must walk your path alone. No one can walk it for you."

I was getting a cramp in my leg; I leaned back and my hand touched the floor. The earth was cool. It was so unusual to be in a house where the floor was earthen. From what I could see, it was packed down tightly so that the surface had become hard and stable—if the room were swept, very little of the surface would move. He asked me to look at the candle again, and when I was ready to slowly shut my eyes.

"What do you hear?" he asked.

I noticed, very faintly, the music of a wood flute. "Notes that blend together to make music. A haunting, serene, noble music that makes me want to savor each note."

It was as if I could taste the notes with my ears. I was totally captivated by the sounds when I heard him ask, "Is that all you hear?"

I had been so into the music, I wasn't sure what he said, and I asked him to repeat his question. He did.

"I hear the most beautiful flute music I have ever heard in my life. It sounds like something unearthly. It's so beautiful."

"Do you hear anything else?"

"No. It's so quiet; my ears are ringing from the lack of stimulation. I'm not used to it being this quiet."

"Do you hear the silence between the notes?"

"Yes, now that you mention it. But I didn't. I only heard the notes.

"Without the silence, the notes would have no meaning. They are husband and wife. They are family. In coming together, they fulfill their purpose. I could not fulfill my purpose without interacting with you, and you would not fulfill your purpose without interacting with me. We have come together to create a harmony you will take with you, and you will teach others to create their harmony."

I was thinking about the word harmony when he said, "Harmony. It is an interesting word. How often do people spend the days of their lives and never find it? They are so busy playing notes that they do not take the time to put in the silence that would bring about the music. Like the darkness surrounding the flame and the silence between the notes, for many people, the darkness and the silence are not seen or heard."

Yes, I was starting to get it. I was musing about the husband-and-wife metaphor when he continued. "You were chosen to come here because you have suffered enough to understand that the anguish and turmoil each of us have suffered is the life ingredient from which kindness and compassion can grow. In essence, when we understand our own suffering, those of us who are ready, feel compelled to help others to understand theirs. You are ready and you want to serve. If you were not ready to serve others, you would not be here."

Okay! Maybe I've suffered some, but lots of people have suffered more than I. Why me? Why was I chosen?

Once again, he responded without my actually asking the question. "Before you were born, you were given a life curriculum, and it included your meeting with Theophane and eventually, me."

As I was still trying to mentally digest the before-you-were-born comment, he continued. "You are also ready to understand the need for light and darkness, sound and silence, action and rest. You are ready to receive the seeds of change, sown in the form of thoughts that can grow and thrive within you. You are ready to change yourself and, in time, the world."

Every time he spoke about my helping to change the world, it gave me the willies, and he knew it. I didn't bother to ask how; I knew he would tell me to wait and that eventually I would be shown.

"As we spend the next week together, I will present questions that, as you answer them, will give you the guidance and direction you need. Unlike most schools, where people sit at desks and face a teacher who provides information they often are not interested in, the information you receive will captivate and challenge you."

He had my attention. There was no question about it; the anxiety I felt was making my left eye twitch. It happens when I'm stressed. I adjusted my glasses.

"Joe, we are going to do real things: hike in the desert, watch animals, smell flowers, sing, dance, play music, talk to each other, listen to each other, share opinions, and, in fact, go about our day in a manner that will not in any way seem extraordinary. What will be special will be the way in which we experience our days together. You will see the ordinary in a new way that will help you more fully appreciate your life and your place in the universe. You will experience a dimension you have not comprehended before. Are you still in, Joe?"

"Yeah." But I knew enough to know that I really didn't know what I was getting myself into or exactly what he was talking about. At this point, the affirmative answer was simply a continuation of my leap of faith.

"Did you wonder why I asked you to come here in the middle of the night and arrive exactly at 4:30 AM?"

"It is strange, but this whole adventure has been strange, so I didn't give it much thought. Was I supposed to?"

"You see what I mean about being asleep?"

"No, I don't get it. What do you mean?"

"Well, you were directed to drive two hundred miles in the

middle of the night and arrive for a meeting at a time when people rarely, if ever, begin meetings—and yet, you accepted the direction and were here on time. You also put your life on hold and spent money for an airline ticket; you rented a car and most of all you were willing to put your life in peril because you did not know for sure what was going to happen to you. You did all this for a reason. The psychologist, Maslow, calls it self-actualization. You are here because you know there is more to your life than running scared, worrying, or hoping for crumbs from the corporate, state, or whatever table it is where people find their crumbs. You know there is more and you don't want to be asleep. So I will awaken you!"

It was true! I was there because I was searching. *Maybe, just maybe, something might happen that would help me climb out of the rut that had become my life.*

He continued, "I asked you to get here at 4:30 AM because by doing so, I started the process of changing your internal clock. When you return to your home, do not be surprised if you decide getting up at 4:30 AM is something you want to do; something you will enjoy and benefit by."

I was listening, but the idea of arising at 4:30 AM did not seem inspirational.

"We will talk more about getting up early as we progress. For now, I want you to realize that if you want something badly enough... you will change. You have proven that. You will go without sleep if need be and take chances that depart from your ordinary desires and actions. All of this, Joe, is driven by your desire to have pleasure. You see, everything we do is directed toward two desires: to increase pleasure and minimize pain."

Calling me Joe had become annoying. I didn't think it would. When he explained that names really don't tell us who we are, I bought into it, even though I didn't like it. In fact, I didn't like being called Joe, but I kept it to myself. I believed he was the keeper of the key to knowledge I wanted, and so I'd figured it would be best to keep quiet and put up with it.

"You do not like it when I call you Joe. It makes you angry?"

So much for hiding my feelings.

"No, I don't; it feels disrespectful. It makes me feel like you are playing with me and I have to play the game or you won't give me the answers I'm here for. I like the idea of getting an Indian name, even though at my age, I should be over that kind of thing, but I don't like your custom. I'd prefer, rather than calling me Joe, that you don't call me anything."

In response, he turned to me and slapped me on my right shoulder with a hearty wallop and said, "So, you are willing to take the chance of my not helping you, rather than be insulted? Is that true?"

Before I answered, I wondered about having to go back home and explain that I was thrown out of the Gifted One's training camp because I wouldn't let him call me Joe. I considered the money and time I had already spent getting there. *Maybe I would be throwing this whole gift, if that's what is was, away because of pride, because I didn't like him calling me Joe. Sometimes, Andy, you are freaking ridiculous. If he wants to, let him call you Mary Ellen. What difference does it make?* But it did make a difference, and I contemplated the times I had lied about my feelings to others and myself because I wanted something. This was one of those crumbs he talked about. I was tired of lying, and if he wanted to send me on my way, I'd deal with it.

"So? Your answer? Remember, Joe, I can send you home at any time during your training, if I feel you are not a suitable candidate."

Now I was angry. Being threatened makes me crazy. Maybe because I don't like being bullied. When threatened, I can feel my game face coming on, as I go into defense mode. Seeing others bullied is equally upsetting and whenever it's appropriate, I usually do something about it. Of course, if Mike Tyson threatened me, or someone in my company, I'm sure my reaction would be different.

An altercation with Mike would be my insurance man's nightmare, as well as mine. I can almost hear him screaming, "No!"

"Well, Coach, too many times in my life, I said something was okay when it wasn't, and I didn't like myself for it. So if you want to send me home, go right ahead, but don't call me Joe!" And I looked him straight into his sunglasses.

This was my moment of reckoning with him. This was my OK Corral, as if we were both standing there with guns in our hands. I was demanding respect. I was talking back to the principal, Mom and Dad, the boss, my wife, and everyone else I should have demanded respect from and sometimes didn't. I was the guy at the craps table, and I remembered Kipling's advice about putting everything on the line and tossing the dice.

The moment of truth had arrived. The ball was in his court, and I was waiting to see what he was going to do with it. I was shocked by his response.

"Andy, I have your Indian name. From now until forever, I will call you Fearless Speech. In Cambodian, your name would be YuWa, and you will learn more about my life in Cambodia in the next few days."

I laughed out loud. It was laugh of relief. I also noticed he called me Andy and not Joe.

"Did you learn something from that?"

"I think I did."

I was still pumped. The adrenaline was doing its job.

"What I hope you learned is that when you fight for your integrity, you feel alive. When you hide your feelings and come to believe the lies you tell others, you begin to grow apart from yourself. In time, some people no longer remember who they were or who they are, because they stand for nothing other than what they think others want them to say or think. They rationalize their self-deceit because they want something: money, a promotion, a corner office, or maybe friendships with people who have power. By denying what they feel in their heart, the price they pay is their integrity. In time, the lies and the denial of who you really are can become the root cause of illness. The body gets out of balance because the mind and body are one, they walk together, and the lies, the distortions, and the denial of our genuine feelings can make us sick. Sick because we are not happy with ourselves. Illness is our body's way of underlining that something is out of balance. It is all about integrity."

I was flattered by the name, Fearless Speech—but I had hoped for something a little different and asked, "Coach, is there a possibility I can ask for a different Indian name?"

"You do not like Fearless Speech?"

"It's not that I don't appreciate the honor. It's just that when I get home and tell my kids, who are now adults, the Indian name, I'm a little embarrassed—maybe something like Wise Eagle would be nice."

"Wise Eagle would not capture the spirit courage it took to confront me. How about Bear? In Japanese, it translates to Kama. I always liked the sound of the name. It is strong. As you will learn, I spent time in many different countries and Kama, or Bear, is a powerful name. A bear is courageous, and you demonstrated courage."

I was thinking about whether I liked Fearless Speech or Bear when he said, "We are spending too much time on your name. My final decision is that your name will be City Bear, because you come from the city. Your daughters will like it."

The tennis match of words was over, and though I had been able to return the serve, he had the home-court advantage, and I knew not to push the issue any further.

"Let us get back to work. I had asked you if you saw the darkness as well as the flame and heard the silence as well as the notes, and though you initially did not, do you now appreciate seeing and hearing more fully?"

"Yes," I answered. But I wasn't sure if I was getting whatever he wanted me to get. *What was the big deal if I saw the darkness or heard the silence? Would it make me a better person? Would I invent the cure for cancer? Have a better life?*

"What do you feel?" he asked.

"Feel? Do you mean emotionally or feel with my body?"

"Both, but you can start with emotionally."

"I feel like a dog trying to learn tricks—a dog who wants to please his master and at the same time wants to bite him on the ankle and make him go away. This is work."

"You feel eager, yet annoyed," he said thoughtfully.

I also felt emotionally drained. I needed a cup of coffee and breakfast and wondered how many hoops I'd have to jump through before I could eat. The room was cool, lit only by the candle and the sun that entered through the window and knew that three hours sleep was not enough. I fantasized about a pillow, a blanket, and a clean, dry space for a snooze. Knowing my thoughts, he stood up, not waiting for a response to his questions, and said while standing next to me, "You think too much. It is time to meditate."

He knew I was fading fast.

"Come with me," he said.

He walked very quickly and quietly. I was jogging to keep up. We went through a small hallway into another room. I recognized the smell of sandalwood. The room was dimly lit with four candles, one in each corner. We sat on what appeared to be a small, worn American Indian rug. I say worn because, like the rug in the library, the distinctive fanny marks were obvious. We sat in the middle of the room in front of a round clay pot, about two feet in diameter and eighteen inches high, filled with sand. Four lit incense sticks were placed in the sand and formed a square.

The entire room was made of all different sizes, colors, and shapes of stone that had been mortared with mud to create a tapestry of rock. Some of the stones had drawings on them that looked like pictographs I'd seen on rocks in the Valley of Fire in Nevada.

The smell was distinct and ancient. I never considered that stone has an odor, but it does. *I wonder if the smell of the rocks is the smell of the universe?*

"It is time to meditate. You need a rest. Much has happened and you are physically and emotionally tired. You need to rest your mind and body, and then we will have tea."

Tea? How about something strong and filling: coffee, bacon, eggs, home fries, orange juice, and toast? Tea? I don't drink tea in the morning, and the thought morphed into "this is not fun!"

"Yes, you will enjoy the breakfast. Now close your eyes. I want you to think of the word *fugai*. It means 'outside the wind' in Japanese. I want you to say it in your mind, over and over. It may become louder or softer, faster or slower; it is acceptable to be loud or soft, fast or slow and anywhere in between. I want you to hear the sound of your mind saying the word *fugai*. Try it now."

I was thinking of the trials of Hercules and the seven tasks he was asked to complete, when I heard him say, "You want to eat? First meditate, then food."

This guy must be a behaviorist. First work and then eat? B.F. Skinner would be proud. Okay, back to work. And I started to say *fugai* over and over in my mind. *fugai, fugai, fugai,* and then I noticed my mind started to wander. I started thinking of home followed by a procession of thoughts that included bacon and eggs, coffee and the morning paper, when I heard him say very softly, "Thoughts other than the sound of *fugai* will come into your mind. When they do, push them away very gently, as if you were trying to push a cloud, and then return to the repetition of the sound. This sequence should happen many times during the course of your meditation today. City Bear, this is important!"

He had called me my Indian name for the first time in conversation, but I didn't feel like a City Bear or any kind of bear. I'm not that big or impressive. Maybe we could change my name to Badger; they're smaller, and I remembered *fugai* and began again to repeat it. When

I recognized I was thinking of something other than the word *fugai,* I gently brought my thoughts back to its repetition.

After what seemed to be about ten minutes, I heard him say, "Gently open your eyes. Open them as slowly as if you were watching the morning sun inch up over the horizon. Very slowly!" After about a minute of silence, he asked, "Are you ready for breakfast?"

I sat there feeling a sense of serenity and tranquility I had never felt before. I wasn't hungry, thirsty, tired, or worried. It felt as if I were observing everything around me but nothing in specific. I felt as if I were a part of the all: the light of candles and the surrounding darkness, the scent of the sandalwood, the smell of the walls, the earthen floor, and the texture of the rug beneath me. I was a part of everything, and yet I belonged to nothing and wanted to bathe myself in the feeling just a little longer. I felt like a kid who doesn't want to get out of bed and go to school on a dark, cold winter morning, a kid who would rather burrow under the covers.

"Reveille with Beverly," he said.

Before I could process what he was saying, he went on, "It is something the soldiers used to say when they had to get up in the morning. It is an army thing. For us, it means get up and have breakfast."

I didn't get the army thing. What did the army have to do with anything?

He responded, again without my actually asking, "I will explain it later."

He was silent for about five seconds and then continued; "To steep oneself in poetry is a glorious thing!" Then he stood up and motioned for me to follow. As we walked through the doorway and down a short hallway into an open courtyard, he said, "Poetry is the perfume of language. It awakens our senses and can engage us. The right perfume can enhance the charm of an ordinary girl and make her quite special."

How did we go from meditation to poetry and perfume?

"Meditation is like poetry. It helps us distill our thoughts into an essence. It helps us focus and appreciate all that is around us that we take for granted. It allows our mind time to rest from its work and rejuvenates us, so we will be prepared."

"Prepared for what?" I asked.

"Everything!"

"How long did we meditate?" I asked, and when he didn't answer, I said, "It seemed like about ten minutes."

I was also interested in knowing if I would always be able to get this overwhelming feeling of serenity from meditation when he said, "Follow me."

What tests await me? I wondered.

"You were really tired," he said. "I know you need to rest your mind and body because of the stress of your trip. We meditated for about forty-five minutes. Often, in meditation, time becomes distorted. Sometimes it seems to speed up, and other times, it may slow down. Obviously, your time in meditation went quickly and seemed very short for you."

As I followed him into the hallway, I realized—*something is happening to me and I'm not sure what it is, or where this ride is taking me. The card and book from Theophane were my tickets to ride, and there seemed to be no getting off until Coach decided it was over, or I quit.*

Chapter Seven

Each life is like a speck of sand that returns again and again to the hourglass that measures eternities.

Appetites

I followed him through the hallway to a garden area. Three huge red rocks, the size of Mini Coopers, were placed in the center as the focal points, and the rest of the garden was divided into sections of different-colored stones that had been raked to provide the illusion of movement. It appeared as if a sea of multicolored waters had frozen and surrounded the rocks. The blue, green, and blue-gray sections around the rocks looked like shades of water surrounding an island, and I thought: *beautiful, simple, and serene!*

He invited me to sit on a chair that had obviously been made from tree branches. The seat had been constructed by weaving together what looked like some type of vine. It was smooth, soft, and had a slight give when I sat. He was already seated across from me on a matching chair. Between us was a tabletop that appeared to be made of a red slate, similar in color to the focal point rocks. The tabletop was supported by legs made of the same type of branches as the chairs. There were no other chairs in sight.

There was no sound or warning before she appeared at the entrance to the courtyard, a woman in her mid- to late thirties, about five feet four and slim; I'd guess maybe 115 pounds. She looked Asian, but the tone of her skin and the shape of her eyes suggested she could also be American Indian. When she smiled at me, my pulse quickened—*perfect white teeth!* I was reminded of my daughters. They both had full braces, and I wondered if the years of orthodontist appointments would make a difference in their lives. Would they get a better job, or meet Mr. Right because Daddy made the payments?

She was coming closer. Her jet-black hair, like coal or a raven's wings, hung down to her mid-chest in two braids tied with sky-blue beaded leather. She wore a loose-fitting white cotton dress with the same blue beaded pattern on her belt and matching moccasins. When she arrived at the table, he introduced me.

"City Bear, this is Star. The name I have given her, her Indian name, is Morning Star. I had heard the name long ago when I was traveling in Japan, where it translates to Gyosei. I spent many years at a monastery in Osaka. During my stay, I met a very wealthy banker who had named his oldest daughter Gyosei. He told me that he knew her birth would change his life forever and that her presence introduced the sun, or as he saw it, great light and prosperity into his life. I thought of the name as a treasure, and after I met my niece, I knew she was my morning star. She found me shortly after I came to the United States. I do not know what I would do without her. She has been with me for about two years."

"Nice to meet you," I said.

She pursed her lips in an embarrassed smile and said, "You must have done something very noble to have been given your name. The bear fears no other animal."

I was flattered and opted for self-deprecation by answering, "But I'm a city bear! City bears think country bears are grouchy because they spend too much time alone and eat berries and fish. City bears hang out in taverns, stamp their paws to polka music, and eat Italian food."

She smiled and said, "City Bear, after I phoned you in New

Jersey, I suspected you would be different. Your description of city bears has reinforced my suspicion."

I answered her response by adjusting my glasses, and before I could speak Coach said, "The story for his name, I believe, you will find quite interesting, but we will save that for another time."

It wasn't the time to mention my thoughts about my Indian name. I figured there would be time during the next few days to talk about it. She smiled at me with her eyes and left.

The silver tray she placed on the table was neatly arranged with cups, saucers, spoons, forks, milk, fruit, cheese, toast, scrambled eggs, bacon, oatmeal, a teapot, a coffeepot, and a pitcher of ice water. Coffee! I couldn't believe it. *Yes! Today I will have coffee and maybe I'll be able to make it through the day!*

The breakfast tray looked like a graduation project from a Zen culinary school. Everything was carefully positioned to create the impression of simple beauty. The strawberries had been cut into thin slices and positioned to look like fans that served as archways under which were placed slices of peach, apple, pear, and papaya. The cheese was thinly sliced and placed next to the crispy bacon and well-done eggs. The oatmeal was served in small yellow bowls that had the texture and weight of stone—very unusual. A lime-green linen napkin was folded to look like a fleur-de-lis and placed in front of each plate.

The breakfast tray was a work of art worthy of a painting by some medieval master. It looked too good to eat; but the growling in my stomach would help me to overcome any inhibitions I had about the artistic presentation.

Coach and I also received miniature ceramic plates, each the size of a half dollar, upon which six almonds were placed in the center and formed the spokes of a circle.

As we ate, I mentioned that the meditation seemed to refresh me.

"That's because you recharged your energy battery."

"Energy battery? Would you explain what you mean by that?"

"Our bodies operate on electro-chemical magnetism. In every cell of the human body, you will find sodium, which has a positive electrical charge, and potassium, which has a negative electrical charge. When our mind tells our body to do something, the thought sends a message to the cells through chemicals called neurotransmitters. These chemicals cause tiny cellular walls within each cell to allow the sodium and potassium to mix and in doing so, tiny electrical charges in the millions or billions of cells involved in a specific action allow us to move. When we sleep, something happens, and we are not sure exactly how it works, but it allows our mind and body to recharge. It is like recharging a car battery by providing it with a current from a wall outlet and hooking it up to a charger.

"That's if we're sleeping. My question was about meditation."

"In some ways, meditation is like sleeping because it gives the mind and body a rest. I say mind and body as if they are two distinct entities—in fact, they are really one. I speak about them as if they are distinct because I perceive the mind as the orchestra leader and the body as the orchestra. In order to create beautiful music, the leader needs to guide, direct, and coordinate, and if the leader or orchestra members are tired, confused, or out of synch, the process does not work.

"It is as if, when we sleep, we recharge by being plugged into power from a generating station. When we meditate, we get our power from the source that the generating station uses. Meditation is a very important part of my day, and I hope you will come to look forward to it."

As we were eating, he said, "I see you have taken in more food than your body needs."

What an unusual way of saying that I was overweight. Did I come here to be insulted? I know I have to lose a few pounds (about fifty); he doesn't have to tell me what I already know!

"You are annoyed at me," he said.

"Yeah, I am. I appreciate the breakfast, but I don't like being reminded that I eat too much."

Here we go again. He's pushing my buttons and I'm reacting. I didn't care. The meditation had taken the edge off before he made his comment about eating. Once he reminded me of my inability or unwillingness to control my food intake, any serenity that the meditation brought had quickly evaporated. I felt attacked and ready to fight back when he said, "City Bear, I am not criticizing you. I am simply stating an observation about a problem that you have not been able to overcome. My intention is to help you, not criticize. Remember, you were chosen to come here before you were born and you earned your acceptance here when you gave a gift from your heart. You are here to receive many gifts, and in return, you will use your gifts to help others. I mention the eating because I know it has plagued you for many years. I mention it because before I can help you to overcome this problem, we must first identify it, agree that it is a problem, and then you must give me permission to enter your mind with my words so that we can correct the problem. Is this acceptable to you?"

I felt like Jackie Gleason in a *Honeymooners* episode, where he gets angry with Alice for what he perceives as an affront, only to find later that she was doing something thoughtful or kind for him. I felt like I was living one of those episodes where he ends up looking sheepishly at his shoes and apologizing.

"Okay, I guess I do look like I'm in training to do a Pillsbury Doughboy commercial."

"There is no need for that. Putting yourself down will not be accepted here, even if you tell me that you are only joking. It is not a joke when you are not happy with yourself. It is not funny at all. In fact, it is very sad, because you are precious; you are a miracle. We are all miracles, and sometimes miracles need to be reminded of who they are."

We sat silently for a while, and I noticed that the sun had risen above the east wall of the rock garden. I felt its warmth on my body. *This is primeval nurturance—food for the body and spirit that cannot be seen or touched, and yet, is substantial and energizing.*

The smell of the desert in the early morning and the warmth of the sun made me feel joyously alive. It reminded me of my friend Charlie, who has passed. He used to say at moments like this, "Brother Andrew, this is a glorious day!" And I thanked Charlie for being Charlie and teaching me to say, when confronting a moment of undiluted sunshine, "This is a glorious day."

And I wondered about the question he asked earlier when we were looking at the candle: "What do you see?"

I no longer see just the light. I see the sun from which all life comes and I see the light it sends to everything that in some way isn't blocked or covered. Though I can't touch the light or capture it and put it in a box, light was—and is—the spark from which our earth and everything on it receives nourishment. Light is mother's milk for the Earth and everyone on it. Light is the yeast of life. It warmed the oceans millions of years ago and created the cake mix that formed everything and us. Light allows us to survive, and yet, until today, I had taken it for granted.

The thoughts about the candle and the sun took only seconds, and yet it seemed as if I was savoring them, like the smoke of a fine cigar or the kiss of a beautiful woman. Again, time in some way had become distorted, and the seconds seemed like minutes.

"You are paying attention. You are seeing the commonplace with new eyes. City Bear, you are beginning to wake up."

And I knew what he meant on a level that didn't require an answer. A level in my being that houses the essence of who I really am.

"So you became angry with me when I commented about your eating, and now, you are thinking that maybe you should skip breakfast, even though you are hungry. And possibly there is a part of you, because of the angry feelings, that is telling you to show me that you do not need my food by not eating or by saying that you will only have some coffee. The part of you that may be whispering this message is the part I call false pride. It is something in all of us that is left over from a time when we were very young and were taught by our parents that life has boundaries and limitations. At the time, we thought that we were omnipotent and the reality check—our parents' rules and regulations—was something we fought against. The residual effects are still with many of us as adults. It is what we do when we pout because we do not like something."

He was articulating the exact feelings going through my mind, and then he said, "I will explain. When we feel that we cannot control people, events, or situations, it can make us nervous. Nervous because in an infantile way, we think we always know what we need or what is best for us. By having our thoughts or desires fulfilled, we believe we are in control. We feel safe. Of course, it is all an illusion—the feeling is still there."

As he was speaking, my mind was scanning my internal database for incidents where I wanted control and couldn't have it, times when I felt frustrated and anxious, and times when I worried because I, in some way, was the hunted and not the hunter.

"Most people are scared, City Bear. They worry they will not have enough—enough love, money, recognition, time. They are afraid of lack. They are afraid they will not have what they think they need. They are afraid that there is not enough to go around and they must struggle, fight, and if need be, lie, cheat, steal, or kill to get their needs met. Is that how you were feeling when you were on your way to meet your editor?"

Thinking back, it was only six weeks ago, and yet it seemed like another lifetime. I was trying to recapture the thoughts and feelings of the day I met Theophane. I remember I was distraught about money, my daughter's divorce-related problems, my family problems, my health, and my work. Maybe twenty seconds had passed since he asked the question about what I was feeling. I broke the silence by nodding my head in affirmation. Everything he said was true. I was worried that I would not get what I needed. I was worried about lack.

He had taken his sunglasses off for the first time since we met, and when I looked up, I looked at his eyes. Until that time, I had never made eye contact. His eyes were a soft greenish-brown, and my immediate impression suggested sadness and concern. They were compassionate eyes; yet I sensed he had witnessed events that would chisel pictures of suffering in his psyche that could never be erased—events that would be life altering and with the passage of time form the foundation for compassion. I know that all who suffer don't always find compassion; and for those who do, the gift is often worth the pain.

"I wanted to give you time to adjust to the environment, this experience, and to me before I looked into your soul and allowed you to see into mine."

I was wondering what he meant about looking into my soul, when he said, "You have heard people say that the eyes are the windows of the soul?"

"Yes, of course," I answered.

"It is true. Our eyes tell others about us. Our eyes tell who we really are with no pretending. Of course, people can look at us and smile, even if they hate us, but their eyes will tell the truth if you know what to look for."

I wondered who figured out that wearing sunglasses gave him or her (maybe poker players) an advantage.

As he was speaking, I was thinking about what I saw in his eyes. My projection reminded me of lines from a Gibran poem that played silently in my mind: *The deeper the sorrow carves into your being, the more joy you can contain.*

Whatever seeds of sorrow had been planted, now, in the fullness of time, had provided him with a garden of joy. *The same fire that destroys the forest becomes the initiator for new life.*

My thoughts were interrupted when he said, "You have suffered."

"Of course. Haven't we all? Isn't suffering as much a part of life as breathing or eating?"

"Yes. But it appears to me that you have suffered more than most people."

"I don't know about that. I don't know how much or how little others have suffered. My guess is that most folks figure that they have suffered more than the other guy."

"City Bear, from the time you were a little boy, you suffered more than most because you always were, and are, a writer. You are more sensitive than the average person because you are creative. A creative person often has higher highs and lower lows than the average man or woman because they see and feel more. Your brain comprehends the subtle nuances of life like an artist understands the complexities of color, form, perspective, and light."

As interesting as I found the conversation, at that point, I had taken only some coffee, and my stomach was making those low grumbling sounds that translate to, "I want to eat now!"

"Coach," I asked, "do you mind if I start on breakfast?"

"Please help yourself. There is so much to do and say that sometimes I forget to eat."

It amused me. *I also forget things ... the car keys ... the car payment ... but never a meal.*

The strawberries were covered with a very light sprinkling of sugar, and I recognized an increase in my saliva as I anticipated the first bite.

"Oh, yes!" I said after the first bite. *Take it easy, it's only a strawberry but it was so tasty, the combination of sweet and sour on my tongue had inspired me to say, "Oh, Yes!"* And I laughed at myself mentally because I knew it sounded like I was in the throes of a fulfilling sexual encounter.

"I take it you liked the strawberry, try the cheese."

The cheese had been cut in the shape of small arrowheads. It was new to me. The texture was less firm than a hard cheese like cheddar.

It had a strong smell, as if it was very fresh, very alive, and it delighted my taste buds with the first bite.

I was about to ask him about the cheese when he said, "City Bear, why do you think you are unhappy? What do you think it will take to make you feel good about yourself and your life?"

I put down the fork. His question had taken my appetite away. For now, the strawberry and cheese were enough to quiet the gustatory orchestra.

"There is so much I don't understand. My mind keeps playing all the old songs, looking for a breakthrough, an epiphany, a deeper understanding. But it doesn't happen. There are no new answers, only old issues."

He was looking directly into my eyes. I looked away and said, "Okay. What you are saying makes sense, but so what? It's not easy to change things. If it were, people would do what needed to be done and solve their problems. Am I missing something?"

"Do you believe people want to or are willing to change the way they think?"

I was working on an answer when he continued, "Before you answer, listen to me. Most people think that if they had the right job, with enough money, good health, minimal personal problems with family and friends, and someone who loves them as a spouse or significant other, they would be happy but it does not seem to work that way. There is always something that is not exactly the way they want it to be. And because it is not the way they want it to be, they are miserable. It happens all the time."

I had taken a sip of coffee as he paused. I felt somewhat dissociated, as if I were watching myself sitting and listening.

"Have you ever thought that most folks might have it wrong? Have you ever considered that most of the things they think they have too much of, or too little of, are actually what they need to be happy? That by working with what they have or do not have, that by participating in the act of living each day with a sense of gratitude, eventually they will find fulfillment in what may seem to be too much or too little?"

I was listening with anticipation. I felt like he was on the verge of dropping a wisdom pearl, and I didn't want to miss it. I was also thinking of those folks who are starving, or being tortured in some third-world prison, and them having what they needed didn't make sense.

He answered my thought by saying, "This lifetime is only one of many for everyone, and each life is like a speck of sand that returns again and again to the hourglass that measures eternities."

His use of the hourglass simile had my mind processing at full tilt when he added, "City Bear, there is something else; we all want to be important. We all want to matter. We all want to feel that our life, the only one we think we have, means something. One of the ways some folks measure their importance is by how much they have, and for some, their lives are spent acquiring more and more because it is their way of measuring their success. Yet, many of those people still feel empty. No matter how much they have, they feel as if something is missing. They feel that they are incomplete—and they are!"

I used the time he spoke to devour the breakfast and was closing in on finishing the last of the bacon and eggs when he said, "I have a surprise for you."

He pushed back his chair and stood up. He was off and walking, and I had to half-trot to catch up. As I followed him, I sensed movement at the courtyard entrance to my right. When I turned to follow the movement, Star stopped for a half-second, smiled at me, and asked, "Breakfast has been satisfactory?" "Just wonderful. And the presentation was outstanding." *I hope she doesn't clear the table.*

She smiled again and asked, "May I get you anything else?"

As she passed by, I recognized the same perfume I remembered in the hallway. Again, it sent my olfactory lobe into orbit. *What a slave I am to my appetites.*

Before I could answer, Coach came back around the corner and said, "City Bear, I need to show you something very special."

As I followed him, we passed the wall of the stone room where we had meditated. On the outside, the stones looked even older than they did on the inside. It was obvious, looking at the weathered shades of mortar, that major repairs had been made to the structure. The wall of the stone room blocked my view to the right and front. All that was visible to the left was desert: sand, scattered low, thin brush, mostly without leaves, some cactus and sky, lots of sky—a perfect blue canvas that stretched all the way to the distant mountains, which looked like speed bumps.

"Stop when you get to the corner of the stone room. Close your eyes and do not peek."

His directions were given with a firmness that I found intimidating. The memory of Star's perfume was still vying for my attention as I listened to his command.

"City Bear, take two more steps, turn right, and open your eyes."

I had no idea and no warning what to expect—my intuition told me it would be something very special.

Chapter Eight

City Bear, for many people, their wildflower spirit is not even a memory, because they have been oppressed for so long. They have forgotten who they are, and they have lost the beauty of feeling untamed and original.

The Gift of the Wildflowers

It was magnificent! Breathtaking! Spread in front of me as far as I could see were thousands—no, tens of thousands—of wildflowers. It was the most elegant arrangement of nature's artistry I had ever encountered.

I have always enjoyed a beautiful garden, but this was more than a garden; it was visual and olfactory dessert. I recognized California bluebells, Indian blanket, arroyo lupine, black-eyed Susans, Mexican hat, and showy primrose. This artist's palette was way beyond anything I had encountered, and I could only identify a fraction of the varieties. I felt like I did when I first saw the Grand Canyon.

All I could say was, "Wow!"

Somewhere in my past, I remember reading the quote, "If a man could get his hands on enough flowers, he could rule the world." And I wondered what had transpired in his life that gave the author the inspiration for the insight.

If the quote were true, Coach could be named king or president or whatever it would be that the ruler of the entire world would be called. Mentally, I played with names. *Maybe Your Supreme Royal Keeper of the Flowers? Nah! Too feminine. Maybe Your Majesty of all that Grows and Awaits Rebirth? Give it a break.*

"How do you like my garden?"

"How'd you do this? These flowers need water. How'd you get them to grow like a carpet for a deity on the desert? I feel like I'm in an outdoor art museum."

The view was down and into a gently sloping, bowl-like valley bordered by a rise in the landscape that blocked the garden from the roadway. In order to see the wildflowers, a passerby would have to get out of the car, walk up a ten-foot incline, and look down. Most people wouldn't do that, because the area next to the road was parched and uninviting.

"There is an underground spring that provides the water. People who pass by do not see the flowers, but some have stopped and asked for water. Usually, their car has had a radiator problem. Sometimes they ask how I can live here without water. My guess is they think I have a tank somewhere. I tell them I have an old and deep well, which is true. It seems to satisfy them. I provide them with water that is a little cloudy and they go away. It may sound selfish, but if they knew the wildflowers were here, there would be bus trips to see them and I would have no peace. In time, some would pick flowers to take with them and destroy the beauty at which they came to marvel."

He sighed and continued, "The flowers are my gift to the Creator through Mother Earth. They are my small way of making up for all the pollution and desecration. This garden is my altar from which I give thanks."

He paused for a few seconds, as if he was thinking thoughts he was not ready to share with me. I was totally focused on his explanation and wanted to hear more.

"City Bear, each one of these wildflowers is different. Though many of a specific variety may appear to be the same, if you take the time to look carefully, they are different. The flowers are more than my hobby; they are my offering to the Creator. Over the past few years, I have spent many joyful hours tending to my garden. Weeds try to choke some flowers, insects and animals eat some, and for reasons unknown to me, some just die. I am the garden keeper; I am the protector of the wildflowers, and in return, they reward me by being what they are … with no pretending."

Here we go again, when he said, "with no pretending." He had used this phrase before, and I still didn't know what it meant.

"Remember, I told you that you would receive many gifts?"

"Yeah, I remember."

"This is your First Gift. I call it the Gift of the Wildflowers."

I didn't get it. Where was he going with this? I was thinking that I had not made whatever connection he had in mind when he said, "Look at the word wildflower and take it apart. Wild means untamed, original. Flower is that which grows and blossoms. City Bear, there was a time that we, as people, were much like the wildflowers. Our spirits were free and we were at one with the earth, moon, stars, sky, animals, and oceans. They were our brothers and sisters. Then, some folks who wanted to control how others thought and acted, and in their minds for the greater good of all, those people started to make laws. It was not all bad, because some people violated the rights of others, and predators will always prey on the weak. Lawmakers, or at least some of them, because they were the best educated, or had the most money started to make laws that benefitted them and not all people. Laws gave them control, and with control, came greed and the desire for more power and control. They also decided who was considered worthy of fair treatment and who was not."

Think of what happened to the Catholics in Ireland, the Jews in Europe, the American Indians and the African slaves in America, and in our own country, the poor. The people who made the laws that discriminated often committed atrocities toward their brothers and sisters under the banner of what they decided was "best" for all when, in fact, their own purposes were being served. Over three hundred treaties were signed with Native-Americans and all of them were broken.

I continued thinking about the senselessness of people being killed or imprisoned because of the color of their skin, or the god they chose to worship, when he continued.

"City Bear, for many people, their wildflower spirit is not even a memory, because they have been oppressed for so long. They have forgotten who they are and they have lost the beauty of feeling untamed and original."

I believed I was starting to understand where he was going when he said, "The second part of the word—flower, to grow and blossom—is also a basic human right. Yet, those same folks who made the laws were also deciding who could grow and blossom. Look what they did and continue to do to the poor in our cities, as well as to countries that have something they want. Ask the American Indians, and most will say that our government continues to treat them with disdain. You probably do not remember it, but there was a time in our country's history when a bounty was paid for Indian scalps. Certainly, the lawmakers who interacted with the Indians, then and now, do not want them to grow and blossom. Again, the origin for these scurrilous acts is usually greed and the desire for power and control."

He was silent for what seemed like a minute as he stared out toward the mountains. I knew it would have been inappropriate to speak, so I waited.

He continued, "So, once we were all wildflowers, but the lawmakers were not the only ones to steal our wildflower heritage. They can also be parents, friends, teachers, lovers, and bosses—anyone who cannot or will not see the uniqueness that is you. They are those who tell us to bury our dreams deep and bang a drum with a stick when there is a violin or maybe an orchestra within us and countless audiences waiting to stand and cheer our performance."

He had my attention. I wondered how many people gave up their dreams because they bought into the system. *Some people like being told what to do and when to do it because they don't want to think. They would rather have someone else think for them.*

"There are those who tell you that if you do what they say, you will be rewarded, because they own the rewards and decide who gets them. Think of all the people who went to work their entire lives and were promised a pension and were cheated out of it, while many of the people who cheated them are living well, outside the reach of the law, because of legal loopholes."

It was true; he was right. An awful lot of good people were lied to, hurt, and disposed of like rotting garbage.

"City Bear, they are those whose eyes are fearful others will get a crumb from the table of life, because they believe that crumb will be one less for them, though they already have more crumbs than they will ever need."

As I was listening and trying to take it all in, I was also trying to think of exactly who "they" were in my life, as well as trying to think of who "they" might be in the lives of others. He paused and folded his hands in front of him.

"They are those who have forgotten that they too are wildflowers who will get what they need from the Creator. They are those who have forgotten how to embrace the heat of the sun, the chill of the night, the fury of the storm, and the cleansing breath of the wind. They are those who have forgotten their purpose: to give glory to the Creator. They are those who want us, like them, to forget."

I knew on some level that this message was directed at me with the intention of reminding me of my birthright, as well as the birthright of everyone on our tiny planet.

"This is my message, City Bear. This is the gift of the wildflowers: do not be tamed. Grow and flower to the fullest and remember who you are. Do not let anyone steal your spirit, and if they have—which I think has happened—do what is necessary to get it back."

I had forgotten about the unfinished breakfast. I had forgotten his question about why I was unhappy. I had forgotten the lovely woman who had captivated me with her smile, manner, and fragrance. My only interest was in attempting to follow his lead. I wanted to understand how to do whatever it was he was moving me toward. I sighed and adjusted my glasses. My mind was trying to comprehend it all, not yet understanding only time and the lessons of the week would help me to "get it" or decipher the full meaning of what he was trying to impart.

He invited me to sit next to him on a patch of sand that overlooked the sea of wildflowers. There was no wind, no clouds, no sounds of insects; just silence.

I suspect it was at least two or three minutes before he began. I was starting to feel uncomfortable with the silence when he said, "We all have a story; it is time to tell you mine."

Chapter Nine

Oprah could get at least two shows from an interview with Coach, and her ratings would skyrocket!

The Making of the Gifted One

"We all have a story. It is the complete and unabridged version of who we are. It starts from the time before we were born, with a thought of desire between a man and a woman. The thought that led to the act of life is important, because it sent chemical messages from the sperm of the father to the egg of the mother. If our beginning was prefaced by a thought of love and caring, somewhere within us, our spirit knows that. If we began as an act of anger, power, or lust without love, our spirit knows that too.

"Our spirit knows who we are and how we came to be on a level long forgotten by our mother and father. Our spirit is also the union of the spirit of each of our parents. The male and female components for the union that creates life have within them a code that gives us our eye color, height, intellect, temperament, and all the inherent characteristics that make us who we are. These same chemical and biological markers carry with them the essence of our spirit, which is the spirit consciousness of the mother and father at the time of conception. Notice, I did not say *act of love,* because the beginning of life for many people had nothing to do with love.

"My story had its roots when my father, a Native American, met my mother, a Cambodian woman, who lived in a small village near my father's army post. In 1968, my father volunteered to go to Vietnam. His unit traveled back and forth between Cambodia and Vietnam. He was with his unit only a few weeks when he found a young woman on a jungle trail who had been beaten, raped, and left for dead. He was carrying her through the dense foliage to a nearby field hospital when he met an elderly man who directed him to place the woman on a slab of rock in a small clearing. The rock looked like an ancient altar.

"According to what I have been told, my father motioned for the man to get out of the way, but the man would not move. Instead, he blocked his way on the path and stood there with his hands, palm to palm, in the prayer position, as tears streamed down his face.

"My father capitulated and placed her on the stone. The old man asked him to hold her hand while he walked around her and him and chanted some words that my father did not understand. The whole ceremony took less than a minute, and the old man told my father to take her. Before he left, he placed a gold ring with a fleur-de-lis engraving in my father's hand."

Coach hesitated a few seconds, and his facial expression led me to think that he was immersed in the storytelling, and then continued, "He carried her to the field hospital and told the medics what happened. The following day, his unit moved closer to the conflict. A few months later, while on patrol, his buddy stepped on a land mine and was killed. My father, who was next to him, was badly wounded in the arm and shoulder and was brought to the same field hospital where he had taken the woman. She had recovered from her injuries and had stayed on as a nurse's assistant. She was assigned to take care of him and had no idea who he was. I was told my mother was very pretty and in addition to Cambodian and French, she spoke some English.

"One day, they were talking, and my father thought of the young woman he saved. He asked the nurse if she knew about a woman who was brought in about three months earlier. When he described what happened, she said that she was the woman. He told her the story about the old man who pleaded with him to lay her on the stone slab.

"As the story was unfolding, my mother was smiling when she found out that he had saved her, but became serious and pale when he told her about the old man. She asked my father to describe him. He did and he showed her a thick gold ring with a fleur-de-lis engraved in its center. She told him that the man he met was her father and that he had died more than two years earlier.

"My father wanted my mother to take the ring, but she would not accept it. She said it was his payment for his act of kindness in saving her. During the next few months, my mother and father became romantically involved and decided to marry.

"There was a monastery only a few miles away, and every day the monks were seen in the early morning in their saffron robes, holding their begging bowls as they walked from village to village. My mother had cared for one of the elderly monks, Minh, before he was brought to the hospital. He, too, had been a war victim, and during his recovery, they spoke in Cambodian for many hours. My mother asked Minh to intercede and request that the abbot of the monastery perform a marriage ceremony for my father and her. My father felt very strongly that the ring given to him was a holy treasure, and he asked the abbot to keep it with their sacred texts. The abbot accepted the ring, and soon thereafter, my mother became pregnant. After my birth, my father decided to stay on for two more years, which eventually became four. Because of his wounds, he could have chosen to leave after his first tour, but instead, he chose to work in a supply center that was one of the largest in the area.

"I do not remember my father or mother. The story I told you about their meeting was told to me by Minh. He also told me that when I was a little more than three years of age, enemy artillery rounds killed my mother and father as they slept. The monks, knowing that my parents had perished, searched for me. On the third day, I was found sitting on a stone slab that they said was an ancient, sacred altar used by a group of holy men who lived in huts in the jungle. They had left long before the monks built their monastery, and the old monks told stories about them that had, with the passage of time, become legendary. The altar was about two kilometers from where my mother and father were killed. The stone on which I was sitting was said to have magical healing properties and was kept secret and known only to those monks who were being trained in the healing arts. I suspect it was the same altar on which my grandfather asked my father to place my injured mother."

I was enchanted as much by how he told the story as by the story itself. His gestures, facial expressions, and timing had drawn me in. I felt like I was watching a movie or a play as he spoke.

"They brought me to the monastery and I was cared for by the entire community. It was like living with forty uncles who treated me as if I was the reincarnation of the Buddha. Minh told me I was spoiled. He told me that none of the monks would say no to me, no matter how many times I wanted to play games that involved me hiding, and them having to find me. I believe you call it hide-and-seek. Minh told me that my father had given me an American Indian name. He called me Little Crow, and the monks pronounced it *Itl Row*."

I had this mental image of Coach as a little boy, running around the monastery, followed by monks in their flowing robes calling out in Cambodian, "Itl Row, we will find you! You cannot hide so good we cannot find you!" I could picture him hiding behind a door and holding his breath, waiting for the delight of being found.

"Minh told me that my mother's father was a well-respected holy man who was said to have the ability to heal the mind and body. He explained that people would travel many kilometers to see or speak with my grandfather, and for some, just to touch his hand."

I was thinking that his story could become a blockbuster movie when he continued, "Minh also told me that my father's father was a great healer among his people. My father had talked to Minh many times about his father and how he missed him. When my father joined the army, it was because he had been angry with my grandfather and wanted to, as they say, flex his muscles. He had lied about his name and age so he could enlist. He was six months too young to enlist legally, and on the space where it asked for his race, he wrote Native American but did not specify the tribe. When my father was in Vietnam and later Cambodia, his heart ached for his family. After being away only two months, he phoned home. When he learned that his father had died of pneumonia, he became physically and emotionally ill. He could not eat, and he wanted to die. He was ashamed of the foolish argument he had with his father, and his heart was broken. His mother had died in an automobile crash when he was in his early teens, and when he learned of this father's death, he felt he could never go home. He believed he could never forgive himself."

I listened and considered: *Oprah could get at least two shows from an interview with Coach, and her ratings would skyrocket. All Coach needed to do was to write the lyrics and include something about prison and a train and he'd have a top-ten country-western song.*

I could feel my pulse quicken as I wondered what was coming next. If there were popcorn, I would have bought the super size with the container so big that when you're finished, small children could swim in it.

"I have wandered a little," Coach said. "I will get back to my childhood. I was taken care of by the monks because my mother had taken care of Minh. The monks believed it was their karmic duty to do so because of their debt to my mother, who had no living relatives. I am very grateful to them, because without their care, compassion, and love, I would have been just another orphan left wandering the countryside, hungry and alone, in a place where there was too many mouths to feed and not enough food."

The picture he created in my mind was very thought provoking, and at the same time, very emotional. The idea of a little boy with no one to care for him made me misty. It was the recognition of the greatest fear we all have as children—the fear of being abandoned—that had touched me.

"When I was about five, the abbot of the monastery, Chen-Tao—his name meant True Guide—was bitten by a cobra and had become very ill. There are many varieties of snakes in Cambodia. Chen-Tao had accidentally stepped on the snake while walking through a field at pre-dawn. The cobra struck him three times. The monks with him carried him back to the monastery, where they attempted to suck the poison from the wounds and treat them with ancient remedies."

My pulse was racing as he continued. "I had come to think of Chen-Tao as a surrogate father. He loved to tease me and would say things like, 'Itl Row, where will you fly today? Why do you not have feathers?' Then he would chase me and tickle me. I loved him.

"When he was carried in by the monks and I saw his eyes closed, I started to cry. I was about five at the time. The monks tried everything they knew, but the cobra had been very old and fat and the poison strong. Minh told me that Chen-Tao was very close to dying when I went to him and placed my tiny hand on his wound. My hand covered all three bites. When I did, Minh told me that it appeared as if a jolt of electric current went from my body to Chen-Tao's, and there was a smell in the room like burning flesh. When I took my hand off the wound, Chen-Tao exhaled forcefully, as if something was leaving his body. Again, I placed my hand on the wounds, and when I did, it seemed as if an even greater jolt of energy passed from my body to his and I went into a deep sleep from which they could not wake me. After the second jolt, Chen-Tao exhaled again. This time, his entire body shook, as if he were struck by lightning. When the shaking stopped, he began to breathe deeper and more regularly and he too fell into a deep sleep. Minh told me we both awoke within the same minute one day later. The wounds were gone, there was no sign of the bites, and I had become what Americans call a 'big man on campus.' Chen-Tao insisted that I take the ring given to him for safekeeping. I was honored and wore it on a chain around my neck and under my robe so that the chain and ring were not visible."

If this healing happened in New Jersey, I could visualize the headline in the *Asbury Park Press* or the *Trentonian:*"Tot Heals Abbot." The phone lines would be on overload as people in need of a miracle attempted to track down the prodigy. He'd have to go into hiding, and there would be a phone call from Letterman and an interview with Bill Moyers. Maybe he'd have to wear a disguise. I laughed thinking about a five-year-old wearing sunglasses and trying to act discreet.

Then Coach added, "After his recovery, Chen-Tao began teaching me everything he knew about medicinal plants and herbs. Chann, another monk, who was very serious and rarely smiled, taught me about healing rituals and how to develop my Chi, also known as Ki. It is the body's energy reservoir that can be cultivated and used as needed. From the time of the healing, I was encouraged and assisted in broadening my knowledge, skills, and abilities in the healing arts."

A second headline could read, *"Prodigy at the University of Medicine and Dentistry of New Jersey,"* followed by a story where the medical students are falling over each other to sign up for a class taught by a child of kindergarten age.

Coach and I had been sitting on the sand for about an hour, and my legs were starting to cramp when I asked, "Would you mind if we walked a little?"

He got to his feet with the same fluid motion I had come to envy. He walked toward the perimeter of the wildflowers, and we began to circle the field, enjoying their beauty and fragrance without stepping on them.

As I walked next to him, he said, "As I grew older, many people had heard of the snake story, and they asked for healing. Chen-Tao was very careful and only allowed me to work with those who had passed his tests. He would allow me only to work with those who had in some way shown compassion or kindness to someone who could not do anything for them or pay them in some way. Having a healing session with me was based on whether or not Chen-Tao thought you deserved to be healed."

As we walked, Coach would point out a particular flower and say that it was the grandfather or grandmother flower and that it was especially important to the other flowers. That they learned how to be flowers from their grandparents. There were also parent and child flowers, but the most important were the grandparent flowers.

I started to become familiar with hearing and seeing things that—in my former life, before meeting Theophane and Coach—I would have considered over the edge but now seemed reasonable. A month ago, if someone talked to me about grandparent flowers, I would have given them a donation and lots of room.

He picked a small stone and rubbed it between his right thumb and forefinger before he tossed it into the desert. It was a small, non-descript gray stone. He threw it with the same ease of motion that I've only seen accomplished by professional baseball players or football quarterbacks.

After the rock toss, he continued, "When I was about eight years of age, one of the local generals had heard that there was a boy who lived with the monks whose name was Little Crow who had magical healing powers. Chen-Tao knew that the man had been uncompromisingly brutal to monks. He scoffed at their manner and dress and was known to beat them with a stick if he encountered them on the road or trail. The man had demanded to see me. He had developed a cough deep in his chest and was so weak he had to be carried to the monastery. He told Chen-Tao that if I would not see him, all of the monks would be put to death by his soldiers."

There's always a bully. There's no escape. They're ubiquitous, like grass.

"Chen-Tao did not want me to see him, but at the same time, he did not want his brothers to die. So he brought the man to me. I remember the man's aura, the electrical life force that surrounded his body. It was very weak, and I asked him to lie down and open his mouth. I took three deep breaths and placed my mouth on his and exhaled. Almost immediately, the man fell into a deep sleep, and when he awoke, the cough was gone. He left the monastery without a word or an offering of thanks. Instead, he told the abbot how lucky they were that he had decided not to kill everyone in the monastery."

The thought passed through my mind about those people in the Bible who were healed and never said thank you. I was lost in the thought when I heard him continue.

"After the general left, Chen-Tao told me it would not be safe for me to stay at the monastery. He would send me away early the next day, with two of the monks who were skilled in the martial arts, to another monastery many kilometers away. He explained that the man I healed would feel ashamed that he was healed by a boy, and he would attempt to cope with his loss of face by killing me and all the monks. When I left, so did all the monks, who traveled to other monasteries. They took with them only the sacred books that contained their teachings. The monastery was left vacant."

Now I was wondering about the man who was healed and his lack of gratitude, followed by the recognition that there are some people in this world who will return kindness and compassion with hatred. I suspected that the general had, somewhere in his life, been treated cruelly. He had been a victim, and as a result, became a victimizer.

We had walked another fifty yards when Coach asked me to sit with him at the edge of the flowers. When we did, many of the flowers were now at eye level, and the perspective was very different. Their varied heights and colors gave the impression of a gathering of people. Some were tall, some short, some brightly colored, while others were more muted. As we sat next to the field, I felt as if we were part of it. Again, I noticed that there were no sounds from insects, birds, or wind, and the silence made my ears ring from the lack of stimulation. I felt as if I was in a cathedral made of flowers, and the sky was the roof and had no ending. We had both been silent after we sat, and he was in no rush to continue speaking.

I had become comfortable with the silence when he said, "During the next twenty years, I was moved to some of the most beautiful monasteries in the world for the purpose of continuing my education. By the time my training was complete, I had lived in Viet Nam, Cambodia, Thailand, India, Tibet, Brazil, Canada, Africa, Japan, Australia, and England. In all, I spent twenty-five years in seventeen monasteries and became fluent in a number of languages. I learned everything they could teach me about healing the human mind, body, and spirit, and I had many opportunities to practice what I had been taught. Word about my gift had passed through the monastery walls, and I was sought by the famous and powerful wherever I went. When I moved from India to Japan, the abbot, in front of all the other monks, held a ceremony, complete with incense, chanting, and the music of the shakuhachi, a Japanese bamboo flute, and he asked me to come and sit before him. I did, and he said from that day forward and for all time, my name would be changed from Little Crow to The Gifted One. I was fourteen years of age."

This is all very weird. No one will believe me when I get home. Here I am sitting next to a field of wildflowers in the desert with a guy who certainly did not look like what he purported to be, listening to a story that could easily make the big screen, a story that defied good sense and logic and yet seemed totally plausible to me.

"I came to the United States three years ago, when I was thirty-seven years of age. For a long time, I felt a need to be near my father. After he was killed in Cambodia, his body was taken back to America for burial. They could not find anyone who knew him. The information on his papers was falsified, and after much unsuccessful searching, I learned that he was buried in Arlington Cemetery in

Washington, D.C. During my years of study and training, I pondered many times about the mother and father I never got to know. They were, for me, a dream that came and vanished. I wanted to know as much as I could about them, and I corresponded with Chen-Tao until he died at the age of eighty-seven.

"In his letters to me, Chen-Tao told me what they looked like. He told me of his conversations with them, and what helped me most with my sorrow was that he told me how much they loved me. How when my father said my name, Little Crow, his eyes would light with joy. Chen-Tao made me feel loved, and as a boy, I remember asking him to tell me stories about my mother and father I had heard many times before. He did so, always with a sense of dignity and purpose, as if he were telling it for the first time. I miss Chen-Tao. I truly miss him. He was my mentor, my protector, and most of all, my connection to the parents I would never know."

Time meant nothing. I had become part of an experience that had totally absorbed me. Thoughts of family, work, problems, health, and whatever else had been important were lost in my desire to hear the story continue. My only concern was the urgent need to eliminate the breakfast coffee, and I excused myself to do so. He stayed.

When I returned, he asked me to walk with him again, and we continued to walk around the field.

"When I was living in Cambodia, Chen-Tao told me that I had family among the Native American people. At the time, the monks had become my family. I was so deeply hurt by the loss of my parents, I made the monks my family and did not want to search for my father's people. It was not until my mid-thirties that my curiosity had to be satisfied."

All those years Coach didn't know his mother's or father's family and whether or not he had uncles, aunts, and cousins, as well as tribal members, who knew his mother and father. How heartbreaking it must have been to be a little boy and not know the comfort and security a caring mother and father can provide. In some small way, I felt his loneliness and fear.

"I wrote to the Bureau of Indian Affairs and did not find them helpful. I wrote to the United States Army, and they sent me what they had, but again, their information was based on falsified data. The only information I had was what Chen-Tao told me and when my father had spoken to him of his family in Arizona, he never said what tribe. Chen-Tao thought that my father had a reason for not mentioning his tribe, and he honored that; he never asked, but he thought, because of the location, that my father was Hopi, Navajo, or Apache.

"On my thirty-seventh birthday, the abbot where I was studying asked that I meet with him. By that time, I had healed people from all over the world; and to be safe my location was always kept secret. To contact me, an intermediary, a brother monk, was used who would make arrangements for a healing. Sometimes the healings were physical, and others were emotional or spiritual.

"At that birthday meeting, the abbot told me it was time for me to go home. I answered that my home was with my brother monks. He told me that I had learned all they had to teach, followed by, 'Your father's people are in Arizona.'"

I wondered why he wasn't told to go to Cambodia, his mother's country, and while I was still working on the thought, he continued, "You have lived in the land of your mother's people; you need to know your American Indian heritage. You need to know more than the stories told to you by Chen-Tao. You need to feel the same earth under your feet your father felt under his and see the same mountains he saw. You need to reconnect to your father's roots. They are your roots."

I was trying to figure out how he would know where to go when he said, "The abbot told me that I would know where to go without having to be told. I asked him if there was a specific tribe I should contact for more information, and he responded by saying that we are all members of the same tribe, but most people have forgotten that."

I was still working on the logistics when he continued, "Before the abbot dismissed me, he told me to go to the land of my father and do the work I had been trained to do. He told me that much would be revealed to me as I surrendered to the Creator. He told me my mission was to heal the minds, hearts, bodies, and spirits of the people who were sent to me. These men and women have been chosen because they will go back to their lives with new eyes and ears and they, because of me, will change the course of the world. They will learn from my work with them to heal themselves and eventually work toward the healing of our polluted planet."

I listened to every word with anticipation, and yet the fragrance from the flowers distracted me. *Better than any perfume. I wonder if the combination of flower fragrances is confusing for the bees.*

During my lapse, he had continued speaking. "I had come to terms with the realization that I had been given a very special gift, but what the abbot spoke about was an awesome responsibility. I did not know if I could do it. I was honored, but worried, and decided that it was my duty to surrender to the will of the Creator."

We were on our way back to the house when I said, "If you were worried, think of how I feel. I'm just a regular guy; I don't have any special talents that would make people want to listen to me."

"You were chosen because you have suffered with courage and dignity and have some idea what it means to be one of the downtrodden. You have been rejected, denied, used, lied to, and underestimated. These life events are common for many other people around the globe and the fact that—despite your many disappointments and heartaches—you have chosen kindness over disregard, and love over hate. It is also your karmic duty."

I was attempting to struggle with the concepts of love, hate, and suffering when he said, "You will be given many gifts that are designed to change you, and in following them, you will change others who, like you, want to make a difference with their lives. When you return home, support help, in the form of additional teachers, will be sent to you. You will teach five people, and they will teach five, and on and on, until millions of people in the United States have learned these truths through your personal training and book. The thoughts in your book will eventually circle the globe, and millions more will benefit, as will our planet. You will receive the gifts from me that you need to do your work. You are the first initiate. We expect two more, and each of them will play a separate yet interconnected role in changing the world as we know it."

Now I was more anxious than I was a few moments ago. I knew I had to surrender, have faith, let go, and stop trying to figure things out, but I couldn't. I felt as if I was on a leaky life raft surrounded by sharks and one of the sharks had just bumped the bottom. I had the sensation of sinking.

We were closing in on the house when he said, "With all that has been shown to you and all that has been told to you, you do not trust. You do not have faith."

I was trying to work through feelings of self-loathing and disgust, because I knew he was right. I hadn't made much progress. He interrupted my self-flagellation by saying, "It is okay, City Bear. Do not forget your humanity. We are all frightened bugs running from the light toward the safety of the darkness, in the hope that we will not be eaten or crushed. We forget that we are part of the light and to run means that we are running from ourselves."

He was right. I did feel like a scared bug waiting to be crushed by someone's shoe.

"Before I was sent to the United States, the abbot told me that I was one of many gifted healers whose work had begun over two thousand years ago. And, that I would be training one man, one woman, and one child to take their place in a long and honored line of those who chose to serve mankind. This will be the first time a child will be trained."

Women! How about that, and long before Title IX, the federal law that guarantees equality for women. A child, Wow!"

"The abbot told me, from what he had learned, there have been many women called to serve and their actions, more than once, changed the course of history. Yes! Long before the world knew about fingerprints and DNA, the book cover given to you by Theophane recorded the identities of all who had held it. Some of the names on the back pages predate the birth of Christ."

I could feel my heart pounding in my throat. I felt nauseous as I heard him say, "The abbot told me that I must work to train initiates to assist in healing the world and that we were running out of time. You are a writer. Long ago, in another time, you learned your craft. When you write your story about your training, some will believe it and some will not. Those who are ready will understand and help to change the balance of power. By that I do not mean arms, munitions, or armies, but rather thoughts that become feelings and actions for constructive change. When you leave here, you can never go back to your old way of thinking. It would be like playing with the toys of your boyhood when you are a man. You will tell your story to the world, again and again, and there are many who will not only listen, they will hear."

My nervousness increased as we approached the house, and he said, "You are anxious."

"No," I answered, "I'm petrified. I'm so nervous I need to visit the restroom again, and soon."

"Surrender, City Bear. It is okay. Just go where you are guided each day and do what you are guided to do."

I laughed to myself about my Indian name, City Bear. I didn't feel like a bear; something like Scared Rabbit seemed more appropriate.

He asked me to sit with him in the courtyard at the same table we used for breakfast. He knew I was beyond concerned. My stomach was doing cartwheels. After we sat, I said, "Coach, I don't know if you have the right guy. Don't get me wrong. I'm honored that you have this confidence in me, but I think Theophane made a mistake. There was probably someone else on the train platform and he confused me with him."

"City Bear, look at me." He removed his sunglasses and again asked me to look into his eyes.

When I did, it seemed as if my eyes were made of highly charged particles that were drawn to a beam of light in his. As if he was transferring energy to me and I could not look away. I felt connected, like a plug in a wall socket that was securely anchored and would really have to be yanked on to disconnect. He was sending energy to my innermost core, the essence of my being, through my eyes. It frightened the hell out of me, and I was about to look away when he said, "You will be fine. Continue. Do not look away."

His tone of voice was friendly but commanding and powerful, like the voice of a general who was used to having his orders obeyed. For what seemed like a very long time (but was probably a very short time), I looked into his eyes. As I did, I felt a host of sensations and emotions, including but not limited to sorrow, pain, loss, hardship, discipline, forgiveness, love, hope, and finally, resolve. His voice broke my concentration and he said, "It is done!" He looked away. I had no idea of what exactly had happened—I knew that in the few minutes it took for him to complete his work, something happened. I wasn't sure exactly what it was and how I would react.

The staring match was over for at least a minute before he said, "You are continuing your awakening, and when you looked into my eyes, I allowed you again to see my soul. I allowed you to see who I am, with no pretending, and when you did, you also saw your own soul, because our souls are all connected. We all have the same origin; we all come from the same place. We are all part of the Power Behind All Things, the Creator. We are in Him and He is in us. When you were able to glimpse who you really are, you become aware that you are quite capable of doing what needs to be done."

I needed another nap. Just trying to follow everything he said was exhausting. I felt alive and energized, and at the same time, knew that I needed to take a time out for the restoration that only sleep can bring. I needed time to process it all. My circuits were on overload, and the nap would shut some of them down for rest and repair.

"City Bear, come with me," he said as we walked toward a canvas awning that was attached to the back of the house. It provided shade for two hammocks that were hung between heavy wooden poles sunk securely into the ground.

"Time for a pre-lunch nap. In twenty minutes, you will feel as good as new."

He climbed in as easily as an athlete puts his foot in a shoe. I tried to imitate him and fell squarely on my rear end in the soft sand. He thought it was hilarious and belly laughed, the same laugh you had as a kid when something really stupid happened. Like in fourth grade, if someone's fly was open and they were at the blackboard, and you weren't supposed to think it was funny but you laughed anyway.

An observer might think the hammock scene looked like something that could happen to Barney on an *Andy Griffith Show* episode.

Then, just smiling, but still enjoying my tumble, he said, "I should have told you that proper entry could take some getting used to. Sorry about that."

"Sure you're sorry. That's why you laughed so hard I thought you'd give yourself a hernia."

"No, I am sorry. I am not just laughing at you, I am remembering the first time I tried to board a hammock, and your experience reminded me of myself. I was about ten years of age. Actually, you performed better than I. My foot became wedged in the webbing, and I hung upside down before my plea for help brought a brother monk to release me. He too thought it was quite funny. Again, I am sorry. I do not find pleasure in your embarrassment; it simply reminded me of another time in my life, but you did look quite silly."

No way. He's trying to hide it. He really did think it was funny, and I was not buying his story that I reminded him of himself as a boy. I was annoyed.

"City Bear, you are now ready to receive your second gift; although you need to rest. We will talk more after your nap."

Okay, but after the nap, I will tell him what I'm thinking—and then I remembered, he already knows.

Chapter Ten

A wise man helps others to see the illusion in their certainties because they watch him smile and laugh at his.

Imperfections and Certainties

The sun and conversation had taken its toll, and I felt too anxious to sleep.

"City Bear, wake up. It is time for your education to continue."

I was still feeling annoyed at him laughing at me when he said, "You looked foolish when you fell, and you are angry because I laughed at you."

"You're damn right! I didn't think my looking stupid and you acting superior was funny!"

"You do not think it was funny because you take yourself too seriously. It is very difficult for you to laugh at yourself, and it is difficult for you to laugh at life and with life."

I was trying to figure out what he meant by "at life and with life" when I heard him ask, "Are you ready for your next gift?"

I didn't answer. I was still angry. *You might as well get it over with.*

"Before I give you your second gift, I would like to present you with your first fundamental. Fundamentals are insights that are important; but, they do not rise to the level of what I feel is a gift. So, your first fundamental is **do not take yourself, or life, too seriously.** There is great joy in finding the humor in each of us, and to be able to laugh at our imperfections and certainties. By certainties, I mean those things we believe to be true, without doubt, that are not always true."

He had me thinking about the times in my life I said I would never do something and how many times, within a short time thereafter, I did what I was certain I would never do.

He continued, "It is healthy and joyful to laugh often. A wise man laughs often because he knows it extends his life. A wise man acknowledges his imperfections and laughs at the illusions he has created. A wise man helps others to see the illusion in their certainties because they watch him smile and laugh at his."

He spoke in a matter-of-fact, relaxed manner that suggested what he was saying was obvious.

"City Bear, only intelligent, sentient beings laugh. It takes brainpower to see the humor in life and the events that unfold as we progress through our worldly experience. People who are severely cognitively impaired have difficulty with humor because of their inability to comprehend the subtle nuances and relationships that make life interesting and entertaining. As you receive your gifts, you will see more and more humor in everyday life. Now it is time for your second gift."

I was thinking about certainties, illusions, and the importance of finding humor in everyday life and when I heard him say "Second Gift." My attention drifted back to him.

"Responsibility," he said. **"Your Second Gift is: To understand the importance of taking responsibility."**

"Responsibility for what?" I countered.

"For yourself, your thoughts, and your actions. When you promise someone you are going to do something, do you do it? Are you responsible for your health by giving your body what it needs to be healthy? Are you a responsible worker at your job? Are you responsible in helping family members who need your help? Are you responsible in helping your community members who need your talent or time?"

"Coach, I like to think so, but there is only so much time in the day."

"City Bear, you cannot be all things to all people, but you can take responsibility for your actions and make certain that you set some time aside for others not as fortunate as you. When you help others, you create a reservoir of good feeling that you can tap into if you need it. Dr. Hans Selye, considered by many to be the grandfather of the Stress Management Movement, was once asked about the best technique for coping with stress, and he answered, 'Earn your neighbor's love.'"

I was trying to picture a reservoir of good feeling when I heard him continue.

"Responsibility is important for individuals, families, friends, neighborhoods, cities, towns, companies, the nation, and the world. The problems besetting the world today are largely the result of people not taking responsibility. For example, if people took better care of themselves—many diseases or conditions would be minimized or eliminated. If the owners or CEOs of health insurance companies paid themselves and their boards fairly and not in the gluttonous manner common to their industry, there would be more money to pay doctors and providers. If companies, before they outsource or leave a city, would remember that the jobs they cut often result in the decay of that city, an increase in crime, and eventually, an increase in taxes to pay for more police, jails, and unemployment. If companies were more responsible, many of your cities in decay would be healthy and vibrant.

"When the rich, powerful, and privileged make laws with loopholes benefiting themselves and the average American needs to work two jobs to make ends meet, there is something wrong. Recently, look at the debacle on Wall Street. Some insiders walked away with millions, while many people will never recover financially. How many of those insiders went to jail? Very few. Laws with loopholes. Where is the responsibility?"

He had made his point, and it seemed so basic. My stream of consciousness continued with: *we are living in a country of irresponsibility, in a world of irresponsibility, and for many of us, in a body we take for granted.*

Coach turned toward me and said, "It is time for lunch."

My energy level and the feelings that accompany an empty stomach brought me in total agreement with his lunch declaration. We walked from the awning area through the entrance to the courtyard and into the kitchen, where the smell of vegetable soup reminded me of my grandmother's house when I was a little boy. It smelled safe and nurturing, and I thought of the dark pumpernickel bread that Grandma served with her soup, as well as how quickly the years had vanished.

Star was stirring the soup with a long wooden spoon, and she took a spoonful and tasted it. She smiled at us and said, "Lunch is ready. I hope you are hungry!"

We sat at the table, and she served us each a bowl of soup that was so thick with vegetables, the spoon could stand unsupported in the middle. Warm pieces of fresh-baked flatbread were served with the soup.

I was hoping that Star would have lunch with us. *She seems so mysterious.* I remembered her bubbly voice on the phone that turned on a syllable and became stern and uncompromising. She appears. She disappears. She moved as gracefully as a dancer as she served us. She seems so serene, so content, so happy, and yet, she lives in the middle of nowhere with her uncle.

The kitchen was, like the rest of the house, simple, practical, and spotless. The tile floor was a deep, rich earth tone brown with golden specks. The stucco walls were painted white. The table was not store-bought; it looked like pine that had been lovingly shaped by a craftsman who wanted it to last. The planks that made the tabletop were joined together with a butterfly mortise-and-tenon pattern unlike anything I've ever seen. The chairs were made of the same wood and crafted in the same style. There were no visible nails or screws.

There were only two place settings for lunch, and my hope that Star would join us, I surmised, was not in the cards. I was thinking that it seemed politically incorrect for her to serve us lunch while she, I guessed, would eat alone.

He interrupted my thought by saying, "Star, City Bear and I would like you to join us for lunch."

She smiled at us, took out another soup bowl, scooped a half-full ladle for herself, and placed the bowl between us. She brought a chair from the foyer connecting the kitchen and the courtyard and positioned a spoon, placemat, and napkin on the table in front of her chair.

"City Bear, Uncle explained to me your purpose in being here before you phoned. You must be quite excited to know that you have been chosen to help heal the world. I am happy you are here, and I hope we can help you to understand our ways so you can guide others and make them aware of the need for change before it is too late. Your time with us is as important to us as it will be to you, and by the way, thank you for your thoughts toward me. Every woman enjoys it when she knows a man admires her."

When she had begun to speak, I had finished my first spoonful. The soup was spicy and just the right temperature. Before she finished speaking, I interrupted and said, "Great soup!" Her smile told me she appreciated the compliment. I put the spoon down and looked at her, waiting for her to continue speaking. Her directness and confidence were engaging. She had my complete attention.

"Please eat, there will be plenty of time to talk, and I know you have much to say. I will feel like a poor hostess if you eat cold soup."

She smiled and began to eat her soup. Coach and I followed, and we ate without conversation until lunch was finished. The silence was something I was not used to. I had surmised by Coach's silence that we should focus on eating and not talk until lunch was finished.

Her comment thanking me about my thoughts and how every woman enjoys being admired had me wondering if I was that transparent or if she had learned to read minds from Coach.

After lunch, Coach stood up and said, "City Bear, I have some errands to do. Star is going to continue your instruction. I will be back in a few hours."

With his parting words, my fantasies took on a life of their own; they were out of control, and the voice in my head that warns me about impending disaster said, "Andrew, come back. You need to get a grip and come back!" My heart raced, and I felt woozy. A second time, this time more firmly, I directed myself to get a grip and stop thinking like a love-smitten teenager. Only at times like this do I call myself Andrew. Andrew is more serious than Andy, and I needed to return from La La Land.

With his directive that Star would continue my instruction, I became the kid who blew out the birthday candles and his wish came true.

Maybe his car might break down in the middle of the desert and he'd be gone all day. Maybe a storm would come up and wash out the road. Maybe his car, because of the flood, would land perilously, with him in it, on the edge of a cliff and I'd have to conjure up superhuman strength to pull it back and save him, as she watched.

That's enough! I mentally commanded myself. *Your fantasy is starting to look like an episode from* Lassie, *and it's pathetic.*

I heard her say, "I know this can be a bit overwhelming," and I returned from my happy place.

"True, it's not every day I travel to a desert hideaway to meet the world's greatest healer, to be told that I'm going to learn what I need to fulfill my life's purpose and at the same time, help heal the world. I guess you could say it's a bit overwhelming."

"City Bear, I know that you have been given two insights or gifts that have been chosen to help you see life more clearly and become more fully awake. I have been given the honor of presenting you with your third gift."

As she was speaking, my thoughts went something like: *she is the most meticulously neat and clean woman I have ever met. Her clothes, hair, and moccasins…everything was perfect and spotless. She appears to be so composed, in control, as if she found the secret to serenity. Her eyes are mysterious and beguiling. When she speaks, her presence is so captivating that her words are like background music.* I reminded myself I was probably fifteen years older than she and I was thinking, as my Italian buddies would say, like a *jooche* (a jackass).

Just being with her, I became energized. My leg had been bothering me, and I had forgotten about the pain. I felt as if I was getting an energy transfusion, the rush we get when we're "fifteen or fifty" and in the first stage of love. When our ego boundaries start to give way and we melt into the all-consuming fire called infatuation.

Or maybe I was at the doorway, entering into a state that I had witnessed in others and described as deep, bad, hurting love. The love that makes you think, *I'm thinking of her, I wonder if she's thinking of me.* It's the kind of love that commands you to send two or more Hallmarks a week—because they're so right. The feeling that thankfully lasts only a few months because that's all our body's electrical circuitry could handle without catching fire.

In this midst of the wonderland experience, my voice of reason had returned and said sternly: *Andrew, you are not a teenager. Focus and act your age.*

But I didn't want to act my age.

The emotional current that was pulling me would not let go. I wanted to hear her tell me about my third gift, but all I could think of was how long it would be before her uncle returned. I felt like I was drifting in a tiny boat without a paddle toward a giant waterfall, and all I could do was pray I didn't land on the rocks.

Chapter Eleven

The robin told the boy that sometimes what seems to be good may be bad, and what seems to be bad may be good.

Surrender

Her voice pulled me from the current as she said, **"City Bear, you need to learn to surrender to the will of the Creator. This is your Third Gift.** I will explain. When you were on the way to the editor about your book, you were nervous. You were worried you would not get what you wanted; that maybe he would try to cheat you or, want you to change something that was important to you. You were tense because you were overly concerned with control. You thought you knew what would be best for you. You thought if you got what you believed would be best, you would be happy. You were tense and anxious because you felt potential threat to your certainty. Am I correct?"

It was true. I nodded.

"Your third gift comes with two parts. The first is that when you surrender, you are more relaxed and open to hear what is being said without the contamination of your certainty. As a result, you are calmer and open to alternatives that may be even better than those you have entertained. The second part of the surrender technique will allow you to go over or around obstacles, instead of cursing or fighting them. Water does not fight with the rocks in its path; it simply goes over or around them. When we surrender, we are more likely to find our way."

I began to think of some problem people and situations that were obstacles in my life, and I wondered if I could think of them as rocks and myself as the stream.

"My people love to tell stories, and I would like to tell you a story I think will help you to better understand.

"Once there was a little Indian boy who was born with a malformed foot. He could not run like the other children, and some of them called him names and made fun of him. He often played by himself and felt lonely because he was different. One day, he heard his parents talking about a great feast being planned. There would be buffalo meat, turkey, pheasant, and deer, but the fishing had been very poor and no fish had been taken in the traps or by spear. Fish were an important part of the celebration, and it appeared this would be the first year without fish.

"The boy thought—tomorrow, I will do something really special and prove myself. None of the men have been able to catch fish, and tomorrow, I will show them. I will catch fish for the celebration. Then, no one will make fun of me.

"The next day, the boy awoke long before sunrise. He took his spear and walked in the dark to the lake. It was quite far, and the sun was just peeking up over the horizon when the lake was in sight. He had told his friends that he would provide fish for the feast and they all laughed at him. The oldest of the boys said, 'How will you succeed, Lame Deer, when our best fishermen have failed?'

"He was too angry to answer. He just walked away. He knew that some of the children called him Lame Deer, but this was the first time it was said to his face, and the boy's name-calling echoed in his ears as he walked. Before he reached the lake, he began to feel weak, dizzy, and exhausted. The thoughts of failure had eroded his confidence, and all he could do was lie down on a grassy patch next to the lake and hope that a nap would restore his spirit. When he awoke, the sun was gone and storm clouds covered the sky. The young brave whispered to himself, 'this is bad. The rain will not allow me to see the fish and I will be unable to spear them.'

"Just then, a robin perched itself on a rock next to the boy. The robin told the boy that sometimes what seems to be good may be bad and what seems to be bad may be good. And the robin said, 'Watch me!'

"The robin flew to a puddle beneath some juniper trees, picked up a worm, and swallowed it. Then he flew back to the young brave.

"The robin told the boy that what seemed like something bad—a storm that would ruin a beautiful day—had just provided him with a meal, and there were more worms left for him to bring to his family.

"The Indian boy was annoyed and said, 'It is good for you, robin, because you are a bird and birds eat worms, but it is not good for me because I am an Indian boy and we eat meat and fish and the crops we grow.'

"And the robin said to the boy, 'Surrender your certainty; it has limited you. You are so sure of what is good and bad that you are unable to see opportunity.'

"'I do not understand,' the boy said.

"'Watch me again,' said the robin.

"And this time, the robin took a worm from the same puddle and brought it to a low branch that overhung one of the deepest holes in the lake. He dangled the worm from his mouth into the water so most of the worm wiggled beneath the surface. In just a few seconds, the robin dropped the worm, and as it did, a huge fish broke the surface and ate the worm.

"The robin flew away. The boy was amazed by the size of the fish. It was the biggest he had ever seen, and the boy remembered the robin's words, 'You are so sure of what is good and bad that you fail to see opportunity.'

"I will be like the robin, the boy thought, I will give the fish what it wants and the fish will give me what I want.

"He went to the puddle and picked the largest of the worms that had crawled out to escape from drowning. Then he took a stick and used a piece of string from his shirt to tie the worm to the end of it. He let most of the worm dangle in the water, and with the other hand, he held his spear. When the great fish broke the surface to catch the worm, the boy, with all his might, sunk his spear deep into the fish. It was so heavy, the boy fell in the lake—and lost the spear and the fish.

"This is terrible, the boy thought, not just bad! The fish has gotten away and I have lost my spear.

"Just then, he remembered the robin's advice: surrender your certainty, or you will fail to see opportunity.

"The Indian boy took some deep breaths and said to himself, 'The water is so cool and refreshing, maybe if I can dive deep enough, I will find my fish.'

"By then, it had stopped raining and he dove. Not once, not twice, but four times. On the fourth dive, he saw the fish still and lifeless on the bottom of the lake, with his spear all the way through its middle. And the fish and spear were lying on the largest bed of freshwater oysters the boy had ever seen. The sight was magnificent. It was a dream come true.

"That night at the feast, the chief asked the boy to tell his story. The chief had heard the young brave's story and wanted him to tell the tribe of his uncertainty, of being scared and disappointed. He wanted the young hero to explain how he had to surrender his certainty and look for the opportunity in his problems. The chief wanted him to tell of his meeting with the robin. When asked to tell his story, the young brave chose to thank the Creator for his abundance, knowing that the others would not understand or believe his meeting with the robin. The story of the robin and the young brave is a reminder to accept what is, while having the mindfulness to create what is yet unseen."

I had been captivated by her voice and mannerisms, as well as the story. I remembered that my meeting with Theophane, which seemed like an annoyance, had led me to Coach and Star. I thought about how certain I was about what was good or bad for me. I knew, at that moment, that I would never look at life and its vagaries in the same way.

"The Indian boy's eyes were opened by the robin. He taught him to stop thinking about what he wanted, and instead to see what the fish wanted. That was the lesson. Seeing what others want may help us to get what we want. It has to start with them, not with us. City Bear, the second part to your gift is this: In order for you to realize your potential in all things and overcome all obstacles, you need to surrender to the will of the Creator. Understand that certainty is an illusion so that you might see opportunities others do not."

I told her I enjoyed the story, and she said, "There is just a bit more. I am almost finished.

"At the feast, the chief placed the boy in the seat of honor next to him. He asked for the attention of all and said to the boy, 'From this day forward, your name will be Wise Hunter,' and the boy was so proud, it took all of his effort to keep from crying tears of joy."

Who was this woman? I knew so little about her and yet we were speaking as if we had known each other for a long time. There seemed to be no games, no ulterior motives, and no manipulation in her interaction with me. She seemed genuinely interested in teaching me to look at life in a healthier, more balanced manner, and she did so with an ease that made me want to know her story.

As soon as I thought about wanting to know her story, she said, "City Bear, I would like to tell you a little about myself."

I wanted to hear what she had to say. *Here we go again with the mind reading. I wonder if she's married.*

Chapter Twelve

*When he left, there was a hole
in my heart.*

Star

"City Bear, four years ago, my father moved away. He was unhappy with the arguing in the tribe. There were two factions. One group wanted to maintain the 'old' ways, and the other group did not. He could not accept many of the 'new' ideas, and he decided to leave rather than argue and have bad feelings with people. He went to live with his brother in New Mexico. My father is very gifted artisan; he makes the most beautiful silver jewelry."

I was wondering why she was telling me about her father, and she said, "When he left, there was a hole in my heart—it was the worst thing that could ever happen. This is when the man I call my uncle entered my life. He had placed an ad in the newspaper for a housekeeper, and I applied. I never thought of being a housekeeper, but when my father left, I prayed that I would be shown what to do, and when I saw the ad, it felt right. I have been here for almost two years. We spent a considerable amount of time getting this house in order. It looked nothing like this."

So, he wasn't her real uncle. Calling him "uncle" was a sign of respect or endearment.

"My father is very happy living with his brother. After my mother died, I wondered if he would never smile again and now, when I visit him, his eyes smile and he seems younger, as if the stress that has been taken from him has added years to his life. Like you, City Bear, what I considered to be bad—my father moving—was good, and what I was sure was good—staying on the reservation—was bad. Like the little brave in the story about the fish, knowing what is good or bad for us is not always easy. The last two years with Uncle have been magical. He is very kind, and I feel that my life has purpose. He has taught me much about the art of living each day to the fullest, and being involved in his mission to heal the world is very exciting."

While she was speaking, I mused once again about whether or not she was married. Though she appeared to be in her mid- to late thirties, she could have been in her forties. She was a hard read. It also seemed strange she called him "Uncle" when Coach and she seemed to be not that far apart in age.

"I know you are wondering why I am not married and why I call your coach my uncle."

Her ability to read my thoughts was starting to feel normal. The experience had lost its wonder, and I figured it was something she learned from Coach, followed by the thought, *how'd he do it? How did he teach her to read thoughts?*

"I received my bachelor's degree in sociology from the University of Arizona. While there, I became very interested in the role of women in various American Indian tribes and published some journal articles. I enjoyed the intellectual stimulation of the university, and I continued on and received my master's degree in comparative sociology. My husband attended the same university, and he majored in business. We met when I was finishing my master's degree. The marriage lasted about a year. He wanted the big city; I wanted a life close to nature, and I also wanted to help my people. I have dated many times over the years, but I have not found my soul mate. My sister Doris says I am too picky, and that is the reason I am not married. If you met her husband, it would be obvious that she does not share my desire for a quality man. By the way, there has never been anything romantic between my uncle and me. Referring to him as my uncle allows me to live here without people talking about the impropriety of a man and woman living together without being married. Though I am sure some busybodies have much to say anyway."

We talked as she took the bowls away and cleared the table. I attempted to help her, but she wouldn't allow it. When Coach returned, he seemed to be in a hurry, and said, "Come with me, City Bear. There is much for us to do."

I thanked Star for the meal, my third gift, and her story. I wanted to know more. I had lots of questions, but they would have to wait.

"City Bear, are you ready for your next gift?"

Before I could respond, he walked ahead. I followed, wondering if I was ready for whatever he had to offer.

Chapter Thirteen

*I was speaking, and yet my oneness with everything
around me made me feel as if everything was speaking.*

When Everything Will Change

He brought me back to the sandy patch on the hill that overlooked
the wildflowers and motioned for me to sit next to him. It seemed to
be a very special place for him, because we had sat there before, and
he said, "It makes me happy to look at the flowers. Before I came
here, there was only desert, and now, a floral blanket that had its
inception in my mind. My thoughts developed into actions and my
actions into change."

He stopped speaking, closed his eyes, and took a deep breath.

Though I was changing the subject, I sensed the subject matter
would be acceptable and said, "Your niece is absolutely charming,
and her story explaining the third gift was very powerful. I'll never
forget it."

"You are not the first to tell me she is very special. Both men and
women who have worked here helping me repair the house have felt
the same. I did not know her mother, but I am told she is very much
like her.

"City Bear, what do you see and what do you hear?"

"In regard to what?" I responded.

"When you look out at the flowers, the desert, the mountains, the sun … what do you see?"

I wasn't getting it. I knew he meant something other than the obvious. I remembered him asking me what I saw when I looked at the candle flame, and I remembered my answer, "The flame, the fireplace, the candle," and then his question, "Do you see the darkness as well as the light that fills the room?"

I knew he was teaching me to look at everything in life in a manner far richer than I was accustomed, and I told myself to think beyond the immediate vista to something more ethereal, more sublime. His instructional methods were making me shift my consciousness.

I hadn't answered for what seemed like a few seconds. He was looking at the ground in front of him, and his expression suggested to me that I should take my time; there was no rush.

As I sat there, I closed my eyes, and as soon as I did, I felt a breeze on my face. To be exact, I felt the breeze on my left check. We were both wearing cowboy hats. He had handed me mine on the way to the back of the house, and it made a difference. Of course, it was the right size. The sun was very hot. My guess was the temperature was in the mid-nineties, and I could taste my salty sweat when I licked my dry lips.

With my eyes still closed, I answered, "What I see is the breath of Mother Earth as she breathes on my cheek. With this same breath, she is saying that I am as much a part of her as she is a part of me. And she is telling me that I will breathe in the breath she gives me that I need to live and I will breathe out a breath that will give life to the flowers, plants, trees, and the oceans. She is telling me that her breath on my cheek is sweet and refreshing, even though it is ancient. She is telling me that I, as well as all who have come before or after me, am also part of every flower, plant, molecule of water, animal, and person."

I was speaking, and yet my oneness with everything around me made me feel as if everything was speaking. I felt as if the rocks, sand, flowers, and clouds were speaking through me, while my eyes remained closed.

Then I stopped. Silence. I wanted to just be. I wanted to just enjoy being part of everything. I felt that had a rattlesnake crawled up and curled itself on my lap, it would be okay. That the snake and I were in some way brothers and that, if the shade of my back provided the snake with relief from the sun, I would sit without moving until the sun went down and the snake decided to find another resting place. I was feeling a sense of peace that was strange and inviting.

My reverie was interrupted by his voice, as he said, "City Bear, what do you feel?"

My first thought was: *intruded upon.* I didn't want to leave the state of oneness that was broken by the sound of his voice.

I repeated his question. "What do I feel? I feel the warmth of the sun on my body, and I feel the earth where I am sitting, and I feel happy and complete."

He waited for what seemed like a minute and said, "Grasshopper, you are learning!"

I opened my eyes and asked, "Grasshopper? Where'd you get that from?"

"City Bear, do you forget that I have spent most of my life as a Buddhist monk? As a teenager, I was not supposed to watch television; and do teenagers always do what their parents or elders tell them? Of course not! All of the young monks wanted to watch *Kung Fu* reruns whenever we could visit a house that had a television. We all wanted to be Caine. The older monks knew. They laughed at us. They thought Caine moved like a pregnant water buffalo. Some of them were really accomplished martial artists. They would make fun of us by saying, 'I am Caine. I am here to help you.' And then would laugh heartily and slap their thighs. They said that Caine moved so slowly, if someone gave him a turtle to watch, the turtle would escape. In the monastery, this was very funny; their mocking attitude toward our hero only made us like him more."

I was amazed that he knew about Caine and Master Po.

"The world over, the young and old perceive through eyes that are the same, and yet they perceive so differently."

I had opened my eyes, and as I listened I knew I was really privileged. Before the sun had set on my first day at Coach's camp, I was looking at my life differently and appreciating more of the ordinary. I knew on some level that I would never be the same, and it was anxiety evoking. I think the anxiety was the result of not being sure I could do whatever I was supposed to do after graduation; I was anxious that I would disappoint Coach and myself.

"City Bear, I gave you the seed for your fourth gift, and only a few hours later, it has borne fruit. The seed was presented when you looked at the flowers and I asked: 'What do you see and what do you hear and feel?' Your answers to what you see, hear, and feel tell me that the process of your awakening has begun and that you are ready for your fourth gift."

It was reassuring that I wouldn't have to stay after class or be tutored, unless Star was the tutor, in which case, what seems to be bad may be good. I was pleased with myself. I seemed to be getting whatever it was he wanted me to understand.

"City Bear, look at me."

I turned toward him, and as I did, he bent down to scoop up some sand.

"Put your right hand out, palm up." I did, and he emptied the sand from his hand into mine. Then he joined his hand to mine with only the particles of sand separating our palms, and I could feel the heat of the sand.

"As the grains of the sand are separate, yet brother and sister to each other, you and I are brothers to the sand, the wind, the fire, the water, and to all things that breathe, as well as those that do not. We are all separate, and we are all one. **Your Fourth Gift: When enough people realize that we are all part of each other, as well as part of all that is and ever was, everything will change.**"

As I attempted to process his words, I thought I knew what he meant about all of us being part of everything, but the change part I had trouble with. I didn't understand how everything would change.

Then he said, without my asking, "Everything will change when enough people change their thoughts."

Again, on some level, I felt as if I knew what he meant, but I didn't have it totally and asked, "How will changing thoughts change the world?"

"When people realize that their thoughts can change matter, the process of healing can begin. When enough people understand that their thoughts about themselves, as well as everyone and everything, are the seeds that grow flowers or weeds, they will be careful about what thoughts they allow to take root in their minds. If enough people change their unhealthy thoughts about themselves, each other, and everything that we know of in our world, we will stop the pollution of the earth, as well as the pollution of minds that causes hatred, revenge, jealousy, greed, and unhappiness.

"It is your job on Earth to help scatter the seeds that will bring about the needed change. If enough seeds do not take root in the minds of others—who will also be expected to scatter the seeds—we will all die. Mother Earth has been poisoned by our thoughts that became wounds, and now it is time to change our thoughts and provide the energy she needs to heal."

While he was speaking, he did not look directly at me but rather over my right shoulder. When he finished speaking, he took off his glasses, looked me directly in my eyes, and said nothing. The expression on his face and his intensity made it clear that what he was saying was important. He looked away, put his glasses on, and said, "Change must come now, and you must do everything within you to bring about restoration and hope before it is too late."

While he spoke, his right hand and mine were still together, and after he finished, he turned my hand over and the sand fell to the ground. We continued to sit, looking at the earth and sky, and I felt that by interacting with Coach, maybe, just maybe I could do it. It was an awesome feeling that somehow I could help Mother Earth to heal. It made me feel holy, as if I had been given a sacred trust—as if whatever existed before was no longer important. As if my life had purpose beyond anything I had ever dreamed. All this and yet I had no idea how it would happen. At the time, it didn't occur to ask the obvious: *how do I help Mother Earth heal?*

"I know this continues to be a bit overwhelming. It is expected to be, and if it were easy to do, you would not have been chosen."

You would not have been chosen echoed in my mind. When I met Theophane, I believed that all I wanted in life was to lower my blood pressure, lose some weight, find a job I liked, make enough money on my book to take care of some fiscal issues, and help my daughters with their life concerns. My former wife and I were speaking civilly to each other, and it appeared we could get past our anger and see the goodness in each other. In truth, we were becoming friends again, and we spoke about our granddaughter with a love that healed and transcended resentments. Though in the eyes of the world, we were divorced, I knew in my heart that I would always care for her and that if she needed me, I would be there. And through our forgiveness of each other, we had become bound to each other in some way more completely than when we were married, and for that I was grateful.

His comment about being chosen to help Mother Earth heal "before it is too late" continued to ring in my ears.

I had composed myself to the point where I was about to ask how this would all happen, when Star appeared. I had not heard her footsteps in back of us, and my first awareness of her presence was when I heard her say, "I have made some lemonade and hope you enjoy it." She handed each of us a tall glass—wet on the outside with condensate—and a napkin.

After she left, Coach turned toward me, and before he took a sip, said, "Star, like me, lives in two worlds. Her mother was Navajo and, as you know, her father was Hopi. There has been considerable bickering for many years between the two tribes about sheep because the Hopi are surrounded by the Navajo. On a map, it looks like the Hopi land is the center of the donut and the Navajo land is the donut itself. When sheep wander from Hopi to Navajo land, the Navajo say the sheep are their property, and when the sheep wander from Navajo land to Hopi, the Hopi say the sheep belong to them. It has been and remains a challenging problem, not unlike land problems in Ireland and Jerusalem, or the street gangs that have become part of American culture. It is about turf."

We finished the lemonade and he said, "We will walk!"

I knew by his manner that something important was going to happen, and I wondered how many more surprises I'd have before the completion of my first day.

Chapter Fourteen

All of your problems and trials have been gifts
given to you to help you become more awake.

A Message from the Ants

We left the sandy hill and walked into the desert and away from the wildflowers. We passed sagebrush, some wildflowers, cacti of various shapes and sizes, and as we walked, he was silent. He looked at the ground where he was stepping, and again I was envious of his ability to move with such fluidity. Then he stopped—frozen, like a bird dog that has spotted its prey and pointed. I did the same. I expected to see a snake or a scorpion or maybe a poisonous lizard. Instead, there was a series of three anthills next to each other, formed so perfectly that, like a connect-the-dots picture, if a string were pulled taut over the exact center of each hole, it would form a straight line.

The ants looked like commuters on their way to work as viewed by someone on top of a skyscraper. Some were coming, some going, some carrying things, some not, but all the ants seemed to have a purpose.

"City Bear, your fifth gift lies in front of you."

"Ants?"

When I wondered what ants had to do with my next gift, he said, "Look at the ants! What do you see?"

Here we go again. I wondered how many more times I would have to answer that question before graduation. Apparently, I had passed the test the last time he asked me what I saw; but I wasn't sure I could do it again. I felt a little nervous and then thought: *this is ridiculous. I'm looking at ants in the desert and hoping that I don't say something that's going to get me sent to Coach's minor league team.*

Then I laughed—not a belly laugh, not a snickering laugh, but rather a laugh at myself for being concerned about not being good enough. A laugh that meant I realized my concern about worthiness was foolish. I realized that whether he liked me or not was far less important than whether I liked myself. I hadn't answered his question about what I saw when he said, "Very good!" Obviously, his mind reading approved of what I was thinking and he followed with, "But what do you see? Stop thinking so hard; try easy. Just tell me what you see. This is not a trick question."

"I see three anthills and ants coming and going. Some are carrying things and some aren't. They all look busy, and they all look like they know what they're doing."

I wasn't in the mood to close my eyes and meditate on a deeper meaning that may involve Mother Earth, the sky, or whatever else he might consider a worthy answer. Then my stream of consciousness moved to Freud's insight—sometimes a cigar is just a cigar!"

"Energy! Do you see their energy?"

"Yeah! They look very busy."

"It is more than that, City Bear. Their energy has purpose. When they begin their lives, each ant is given their life's work. Some are queens; their task is to lay eggs and produce offspring. Some are workers; these are wingless sterile females, and they supply food and build. Periodically, swarms of new queens and males called alates are produced, usually winged, which live until they mate. The males die shortly thereafter, while the surviving queens either form new colonies or occasionally return to the old one. Ants are assigned their role in the colony and do not have a choice. They know what they were born to do, and there is no choice. As you know, people are very different because they are not given their job at birth; they have a choice."

It was hot. I have heard people say that because the air is dry in the desert, the heat is more bearable than where it's hot and humid. Desert heat, for me, feels like a sauna, while the humid heat feels like a steam room. The relief from the hat and the glass of lemonade had worn off, and I was ready for a bucket—or maybe a swimming pool—of lemonade. I wanted to get out of the heat, but I knew we were not finished with the ants. I was sure the ants had a very special message for me, and I was hoping that it would come by e-mail and not Pony Express when he said, "Do you know your purpose, City Bear?"

"I'm not sure."

"How do you know that what you are doing is what you are meant to do?"

"I don't!" I answered.

"Your purpose was written before you were born and, like the ant, you have done what you were sent here to do—unlike the ant, whose purpose is very limited, you are here to learn. Everything in your life has been your coursework, your individual curriculum. Some lessons have been learned and some have not. The lessons that have not been learned will be presented again and again until you learn what you need."

"How do I learn what I need? Why am I so uptight all the time? Why don't I feel at peace? Why do I feel like a gerbil running on a wheel and going nowhere? Why does it feel like nothing, or very little, seems to go the way I want it to?"

"City Bear, do you remember when I told you that you were asleep and that some people are more asleep than others?"

"Yeah."

"The reason I ask you again is to help you understand that all of your problems and trials have been gifts given to you to help you become more awake. The difficulties help us to understand others and ourselves. They are the seeds that can become wildflowers or weeds, but more, they are the seeds that allow us to grow to become who we really are, with no pretending."

With no pretending—there it was again, But my mind was racing. I believed that our problems could be teaching tools, and I didn't understand how my challenges could help me to know my job on Earth. It didn't compute.

Then he reached down and interrupted the path of an ant, and it walked over his fingers. He asked me to place my hand in the sand about a foot from the anthill to my left. He placed his hand with the ant on it next to mine so that the ant walked from his hand to mine. My hands were sweaty, and after what appeared to be some brief exploration, the ant walked from my hand to the anthill. Coach asked me not to move my hand, and in less than a minute, a file of ants was heading directly toward my hand from the anthill. Apparently, they were in search of water, and I was recognized as a source.

"City Bear, you can gently brush them off now."

I did, and as we stood there he said, "You are almost ready for your fifth gift. But first, like the ant who brought back the message that water is nearby, your time here will allow you to bring back a message to all people, and it will be done through your book. And the book will be discussed on the Internet, and in a short time, the people who need to hear the message will receive it and the change will begin. **Your Fifth Gift is: Everything you have done up until now has been in preparation for everything that you have the potential to do.** And it is the same with everyone. By the time you leave, your mission will be very clear."

So this was it! I am an ant, and the people of the world are ants, and the message I bring will help the other ants to make the world a kinder and gentler anthill in the cosmos.

We had walked about a half hour from the house, and on the way back, neither of us spoke. The silence felt comfortable. In fact, it felt right, as if the silence was a prerequisite for my next gift.

As we approached the house, he said, "I know when you came here you were worried about your health. Specifically, you were worried about your weight and blood pressure. Before you begin your work helping to heal Mother Earth, I am going to help you heal yourself. I know that for people who have this problem, it seems almost impossible to lose weight and keep it from returning. I am going to give you some of the most powerful techniques that exist to lose weight and maintain the loss. Once you master these tools, you will understand their power. In order for me to help you, I would like you to read a story that I have left for you in your room, on the desk. I think you will find it both amusing and poignant. It holds part of the secret to your health and weight loss, so read it carefully. It was written by a brother monk."

Wow! If this works, I'll make millions. The secret to weight loss! I'll be on every major talk show, and Richard Simmons will call me and invite my mother and me to his birthday party on his yacht. I won't want to go, but my eighty-five-year-old mother will insist, and she and Richard will become best friends, and I'll be left alone eating a slice of his dietetic birthday cake on a paper plate with a plastic spoon. Do you see how easy it is for me to get carried away and go over the edge?

A few seconds later, I was in recovery from my mini-midlife crisis and thought: *get real!* The little man in my brain who silently speaks to me in times of emotional duress had scolded me, and I successfully returned from my fantasy by the time we got back to the house.

I was about to go to my room when Coach said, "City Bear, each day you will be given information that needs time to process, so for the rest of the week, meditation will be at 5 AM in the stone room, yoga exercises will follow by the hammocks at 6:00, weight training at 6:30 and breakfast at 7:15, lunch at noon and dinner at 6 PM. You will have an opportunity for aerobic exercise during the day. I suggest you keep a journal and record your thoughts and feelings nightly before you retire. The journal will be very important to you as a reference and resource after you return home. We will continue our work after dinner."

He didn't say anything about stretching exercises or weight training until now. What a bummer if I don't get to save the world because I can't touch my toes or do jumping jacks.

I hadn't really paid attention before, but the wooden desk and chair in my room looked Quaker or Shaker. I can't tell the difference, but I recognized the look—stark and functional. I decided not to open the manila folder on top of the desk and instead took a robe with me and headed down the hall to the shower. The cold water was invigorating. After I dried off, I put on a fresh set of clothes.

I walked to the desk and opened the folder. On the first page, it read in machine-like script that had been written with a fountain pen:

Dear City Bear,

I have enclosed a story that was written by a monk who came to live with us in Thailand after living a life of crime. He was from your neighboring state, New York, and was what they call "a made man." His specialty was the use of a baseball bat to persuade borrowers to repay their loans to his organization. He was very successful, and his financial good fortune allowed him to keep two racehorses at a stable in Colts Neck, New Jersey. His name is Anthony, and he had the misfortune of using his baseball bat on one of his supervisors who refused to pay him for some work. I say misfortune because the man he hit expired and Anthony became a wanted man.

He fled to Europe, Australia, and finally Thailand, where one of our monks found him in a marketplace, looking exhausted and tired. He came to us in 2002, and everyone who gets to know him loves him. On Thursdays he makes meatless spaghetti sauce, and because Italian food was a novelty at our monastery, he became very popular. When he first arrived, he weighed over 300 pounds and now he is about 170.

This is really out there! A mob guy on the run from New York becomes a monk and I'm going to read a story he wrote that is going to help me lose weight. What a great title for a book, The Mafia Monk's Guide to Weight Loss: It's an Offer you Can't Refuse!

The letter continued: Anthony is very intelligent. Do not dismiss him because of his background. He has much to offer and has wonderful insights into life. He has become a very holy man even though he still carries a gun and says he would not feel right without it. I hope you are able to find the message in the story.

Best wishes,
Coach

Chapter Fifteen

Everything has a price, and the chips, as
he called them, have taken my life.

Kidnapped by the Mob, by Anthony the Monk

Once there was a very heavyset young man who loved chocolate chip cookies. He loved them more than he loved anything in the world. He thought about chocolate chip cookies; he dreamed about them; he knew which cookies had the most chocolate chips in them, and he prided himself on being able to define the difference between a good chocolate chip cookie and a great one. He was a cookie connoisseur.

How heavy was he? Well, on a sunny day, if you got on his shadow side at the beach while he was standing, he could shade a family of four. I'm not trying to make light of something sad, but as Harold the cookie expert liked to say, "Everything has a price, and the chips, as he called them, have taken my life."

Harold had always been overweight, and in the fourth grade, his mother had to take him to the men's department to buy clothing. Other kids would play ball or run after each other while young Harold would spend his free hours with cookie tins and batter recipes. He was the Thomas Edison of chocolate chip cookies—always experimenting, always inventing; he was searching for the ultimate chocolate chip cookie.

The worst thing about being a cookie junkie is that it shows. You get fat. Think about it: people who have shoe fetishes or sexual problems aren't easy to identify. How would you know unless they started kissing your Johnston-Murphy shoes or looked with lust at your great-grandmother? You can't tell.

One day, Harold decided to lose weight, and he went on a diet. It lasted about an hour, until the coffee cart came by at work. Maybe you guessed it. The chocolate chip cookie on the cart could not be shunned. It was no contest. The score: Diet: 0, Chocolate Chip Cookies: 1.

But Harold really wanted to lose weight, or at least he said he did.

He tried all the diets known to mankind and they didn't work. Maybe it's my glands; he thought. So he went to the medical doctor. They gave him a lot of tests to find out why he was so overweight. They thought they found it. Maybe his thyroid gland wasn't working properly, and so the doctor gave him pills. They didn't seem to work, and he was told to increase the dosage. That didn't work either.

Then he wondered: maybe it's psychological. That's why I'm heavy! It's psychological. So Harold went to a psychologist, who thought he had the answer. You see, Harold didn't get enough love as a child, and as a result, he has an unmet oral need. That's why he eats so much. Also, Harold was a middle child, and as is often the case with middle children, he felt kind of lost. He wasn't the oldest and he wasn't the baby.

Harold liked understanding why he was fat, and he thanked the psychologist, paid the fee, and felt it wouldn't be long before he'd be wearing trim-fit Levi's jeans and cowboy boots.

Harold and I have the same Levi fantasy. What were the chances?

Well, he was in for a big letdown, because during the next month, he gained two pounds.

Religion, that's what I need, thought Harold. I'll get religion and that will make me thin. So he went to his pastor and asked for his advice. The pastor, a very wise man, said, "God will help us, Harold, but we also must help ourselves. If God did it all, we wouldn't learn anything." Harold knew it was going to be tough, but he hadn't planned on anything like this. It seemed that everyone had a different answer to his question, "Why am I overweight? Why can't I overcome my need for chocolate chip cookies?"

Harold didn't give up on the religion and started looking for the patron saint of heavy people, but he couldn't find him or her. And he thought, as any logical person would, maybe when the saints were around, there weren't any portly people. He remembered being called portly by an elderly aunt who lived in Connecticut. This lady was a little rigid and somehow was able to speak while hardly moving her lips. It looked as if she was always clenching her teeth. Like she had been shot with an arrow in an Indian raid, and the trail boss told her to bite down on a stick as he tried to remove it.

Harold's mother begged him to lose weight. She told him if he lost 150 pounds, she would make him a really great meal. Harold asked her if he could trade the meal for chocolate chip cookies. She said, "I don't see why not!" Harold's mother was what is called an enabler.

His friends begged him to lose weight. They were afraid he was going to die. He tried, but again nothing worked.

One day, his older brother was kidnapped by the mob. He knew who it was because there was a note left under the front door that read, "There's a shortage of chocolate chip cookies in the world and we want all of dem. Do ya understand? All of dem. If ya eat one chocolate chip cookie, we'll kill your brother. Don't even think of cheatin. We'll know." It was signed: THE MOB.

Immediately, Harold lost his taste for the beloved cookies. In fact, he couldn't stand the sight of them. When he thought of chocolate chips, he thought of those monsters putting a knife to his brother's throat. The notes kept coming from all over the world. Apparently, they were moving him to avoid detection. Harold thought: the bastards!

Two years later, Harold's brother arrived at his door, looking spiffy in his tailored, dress U.S. Marine uniform. By that time, Harold was trim and wearing those Levi dungarees and boots he had dreamed about.

Harold asked his brother, "Why?"

His brother said, "Because I love you."

The End.

I got the intent of the story: love was stronger than chocolate chip cookies. Unfortunately, I hadn't figured out how it could apply in my case, and I was weary. I decided to take a short nap, and before I drifted off, my thoughts found their way back to Star. I suspected that, in some way, she would become part of my future.

Each of the three bells was tapped three times and then, silence. There was no knock at the door and no tea, and after the first three rings, I was awake and mumbling to myself, "Where'd I put my watch?"

I got myself together, headed for the bathroom, washed my hands and face, brushed my teeth, and combed my hair. *I'm lucky; my DNA included the gene for good hair. I wonder if Star thinks I have nice hair.* I shook my head at the last thought and mumbled loud enough for me to hear it, "You need help! You need psychiatric assistance."

After the self-chastisement, I turned off the bathroom light and headed toward the kitchen. Coach and Star were seated and involved in conversation. I said, "Thanks for the bells."

"City Bear, your snoring was very interesting. It sounded like a freight train gaining speed as it raced down a mountain, and then it would stop for a few seconds and begin over again."

"I have sleep apnea." But I was embarrassed that Star had heard these railroad sounds, and I felt like a kid who spilled soda on his pants and everyone who sees him thinks he peed himself. Being around Star made me feel very self-conscious. When I was eleven and wouldn't walk next to my mother in the mall—like many kids that age, I walked about ten steps behind her, so if someone saw me, it wouldn't look like my mother was taking me to buy clothes. It's a developmental thing; all my friends were the same. Going with your mother to get clothes was not cool, and we wanted to be cool, very cool.

Dinner included a piping hot potato soup, cheese, mixed vegetables, and water. It was the lightest of our three meals. I was thinking about how breakfast had been the meal with the most calories when Coach said, "Part of your program for weight loss will include having your largest meal in the morning, a smaller meal at noon, and your smallest meal at dinner. You will also have a small snack at about 10 AM, another at 3 PM, and finally a snack at about 7 PM. You will also drink at least eight eight-ounce glasses of water a day at home. Here you will drink ten because of the heat."

This is interesting—smaller meals as the day progresses and snacks in between. We hadn't had any snacks, and as I wondered why, he said, "Star and I have finished all the snacks, and after lunch today I had to go into town and replenish our stores, while I take care of some business. Tonight, Star will put your snacks out on the counter next to the refrigerator. They will include small servings of fruit, nuts, and hard goat cheese. Help yourself."

Goat cheese? Then I remembered breakfast. It was good!

"You will not be disappointed. It is very tasty."

During dinner, Coach asked me what I thought about the story. I told him that Anthony sounded like a memorable character and that the story's message was Harold's love for his brother was greater than his love for chocolate chip cookies. That only love had the power to heal Harold.

"City Bear, you are correct, but there is more. Where there is great love, miracles happen. If you want to gain control of your eating, think of someone you love who has a serious problem and say to the Creator, 'Thy Will be done; however, I will not eat certain foods that I enjoy that are not healthy for me,' as a sacrifice, in the hope that the problem the person you love has will be removed or resolved. After you say it, write it down and keep it with you. Read it during the day: before breakfast, lunch, and dinner. When you think of eating a particular food that you know is not good for you, or eating something other than your snack between meals, think of the person in pain and decide. Self-discipline can be a wonderful expression of love."

I liked what he had to say and wondered: *what if I keep my part of the bargain and nothing happens? What if the Creator's plan for that man, woman, or child is that their circumstances or health will not improve?*

"Then you have given them your greatest gift, the gift of your love, and it will be recognized by the universe for all eternity and help repay your Karmic debt. Love is never wasted."

I was trying to process his answer, as well as decide who I knew had the most painful life challenge, when he asked me to accompany him outside. I followed his lead to the sandy hill overlooking the wildflowers.

Once again, he invited me to sit next to him and said, "I am going to provide you with another tool, in addition to Anthony's story. With your permission, I would like to hypnotize you and give you weight-loss suggestions that will be very effective."

"Sure!"

"I want you to focus on something you see in the distance in the desert. Do not look at anything other than the focus point."

The sun was an hour or so from setting and the temperature cooler. I looked out toward the desert and decided to focus on a large cactus.

"Okay, I've got it," I said.

"I am going to count from one to ten, and somewhere in between, you decide, your eyes will feel very heavy and you will close them."

He started counting—one, two, three, four, five...

At about five, I closed my eyes, and after we got to ten, I remember listening to his voice telling me to imagine that I was going down a flight of stairs, and after doing so, to think of myself resting in a large, overstuffed easy chair. The next words I remember were, "When I count to three, you will open your eyes and feel wide awake and refreshed. You will remember everything I spoke to you about without trying, and my words will become indelibly inscribed in your subconscious mind. You will sleep easily, healthfully, and peacefully tonight and remember all the positive suggestions I gave you without trying."

I opened my eyes and said, "After I sat down in the easy chair, I don't remember you saying anything."

"Your subconscious mind remembers everything. It is much more powerful than your conscious mind that has kept you from changing your eating habits. You will start eating more healthfully immediately, and it will feel natural. The suggestions I planted in your subconscious will give you the control you want and need."

Wow, I feel really relaxed! I wonder how long we've been sitting here?

He responded without my asking, "Our session took about forty-five minutes, and you were a very good subject."

What a weird word, subject. I was thinking about subject when he said, "City Bear, we are finished for today. Though the hypnosis has refreshed you, you need time alone to write in your journal and review the day before you prepare for sleep."

He was right. I was very relaxed, and I felt awake. I also wanted to be by myself to sort through the events of the day. I went back to my room and pulled the chair over from the desk so that I could sit and rest my feet on the bed. It felt great, and I just sat there thinking. After about a half hour, it was beginning to get dark outside, and I decided to wash up and memorialize my day in the journal he had provided.

Day One

Today has been the most unusual day of my life. I keep wondering if I'm dreaming, because it all seems so strange. Coach is an enigma.

He could be a prizefighter, a horse wrangler, a truck driver, a scientist, a philosopher, or a saint—he's unlike anyone I've ever met, and I enjoy his company.

Star makes me anxious. I know I could fall in love with her, and I have to keep reminding myself that's not the purpose of my visit. More than once today, the lyrics from the country-western song, "Heaven's Just a Sin Away," have reverberated in my mind.

Today, as part of my training, I have been given one fundamental and five gifts. They are:

Fundamental to my success is for me not to take life or myself too seriously. A wise man acknowledges his imperfections and laughs at the illusions he has created.

Gift One

The gift of the wildflowers—we are all meant to have a part of us that remains wild and untamed. If we have lost our spirit, we must do what is necessary to get it back. The first step in doing so is to identify who the spirit thieves are, or were, and make those changes in our lives that return our joy. In our search for ourselves, we must not violate the rights of others.

Gift Two

We must understand the importance of taking responsibility and recognize what happens when individuals, communities, businesses, and nations do not do so.

Gift Three

We must surrender to the will of the Creator and seek opportunities in our problems. What seems to be bad may be good, and what seems to be good may be bad.

Gift Four

We are brothers to the sand, the wind, the water, and the fire. When enough people realize that we are all part of each other, as well as all that is and ever was, everything will change.

Gift Five

Everything you have done up until now has been in preparation for everything that you have the potential to do.

I was beginning to drift off and decided to call it a day. I dated the entry and closed the journal.

Chapter Sixteen

Every dream comes with a price tag. You have to be willing to do things, on a regularly scheduled basis, that most people will not do.

The Ancestors Speak

At first, the tinkling of the bells seemed faint and far away. I wondered if I was dreaming. Then I heard footsteps and the creaking of floorboards. The bells sounded again, right outside my door, and my heart pumped faster. Knowing she was there was thrilling, like the anticipation of a roller coaster ride, as you cranked up the incline. But, there was no knock at the door, no tea, and I wondered if she had read more of my thoughts than I would be comfortable with as the floor creaked with her departing steps.

My watch read 4:31, and I knew I had a half hour before meditation. After the shower and shave, I wanted a cup of coffee, but there wasn't enough time. I didn't want to be late, and it was five minutes to five.

When I got to the stone room, Coach was already seated. I sat next to him in silence, closed my eyes, and smelled the sage. My guess is that we sat for about fifteen minutes before he spoke.

"City Bear, have you ever watched a sporting event where a player is trying too hard and they miss the shot or fail to score? The challenge involves something that they know how to do but cannot because they do not trust themselves to do what is required. They are trying so hard, they are tight in their execution and they do not get the results they want."

"I've seen it happen lots of times, Coach."

"The opposite is the person who, in the same sporting event, looks calm and focused and is ready to do what needs to be done to succeed, because they have practiced it thousands of times and now it is just of matter of letting it happen at the appropriate time. Instead of trying hard, they try easy and they make it look easy because their actions are the result of the unfolding of a body and mind picture that has been formulated, produced, and practiced over and over, until it is accomplished automatically without thought.

"I used to love to watch the NFL quarterback Joe Montana, who played for the San Francisco Forty-niners. When his team was losing, the score was close, and time was running out, he was at his best. He became a machine, a winning machine. He never looked ruffled or hurried. He was a general who could march his team down the field with watch-like precision. Opposing teams, when the score was close, knew his reputation, and some of them became nervous. As soon as that happened, he had the edge, because they began trying too hard and were not able to think or react as quickly as he. It was captivating! Joe was a master at trying easy, and many of the monks, old and young, on those rare occasions when they got to watch TV, admired him. I think part of it was also his name … Joe Montana … what a great name! Very cool."

I had created a picture in my mind of a group of monks, young and old, sitting in front of a TV and cheering for Joe, and I wondered if they could pronounce the J or if their cheers would sound like, Go Yo! Go Yo! I realized I was amusing myself when I heard him continue.

"The older monks generally did not like American football. The only shows I remember they liked were cartoons—especially if there were mice being chased by cats. That was very funny stuff for the old ones."

"It sounds to me that, in some ways, the older monks were childlike."

"No, not at all! They could be very serious and demanding. It is just that they enjoyed simple things and found humor everywhere. They were not fearful of appearing silly or foolish, and they were far more in touch with their thoughts and feelings than most people. Being in their presence made us want to emulate them. They were great fun to be with and very kind. As I mentioned, some were highly skilled in the martial arts and could do amazing things."

"Like what?"

"One monk could split a twelve-inch block of ice by be putting his hand on it. Another was very well known for catching arrows that were shot from a huge bow. One monk in his eighties could hold his breath underwater for over five minutes. Amazing!"

I was impressed, and I believed what Coach was saying about their abilities was not an exaggeration.

"City Bear, before we have breakfast, I want to continue our work from yesterday. Come with me."

I accompanied him to the workout area and followed his instructions for stretching and physical training, and by the end of our session, I was totally spent. I remember thinking that *if I don't eat soon; I'm going to pass out!* When he said, "Breakfast will be in fifteen minutes."

The table was set when I got there. Star never appeared and Coach never mentioned anything about her. We ate in silence until he said, **"City Bear, it is time for your Sixth Gift: Try easy!** On your way to your dream, try easy. In order to get to the place where you can try easy, you have to have mastered the job, the sport, or the task. If you try easy but have not put in the time or the effort, you will not succeed. It is about paying your dues. Every dream comes with a price tag. You have to master the fundamentals; you have to be able to perform without thinking. Then you can try easy and watch it work. It is magical."

"So, to make my dreams come true, I have to decide what it is that I really want to do with my life and then do whatever it takes to make it happen, including learning to try easy!"

"Close, but it is more than that. You have to be willing to do things, on a regularly scheduled basis, that most people will not do. You have to go the extra mile and sometimes an extra ten miles, hundred miles, or thousand miles. You must joyfully embrace whatever it is that others cannot or will not do to achieve your goal. It is about loving the discipline. In order to achieve your dream, especially if it involves something that others also desire, you must earn it. You are in a contest. Many times, the man or woman who realizes his or her dream is not the most handsome, the prettiest, or the smartest. He or she is the person who wants it the most, embraces the work, and takes action."

He stopped speaking for a few seconds, took a deep breath, and continued, "For example, Tiger Woods has a work ethic that impresses the other professional golfers. His practice sessions, as well as his mental and physical training, are legendary. Other golfers tell stories about how he prepares for his tournaments with a sense of awe in their voices."

"Coach, it sounds like in order for me to realize my dreams, according to your recipe for success, I have to become unbalanced to the point of being obsessive?"

"Working diligently and being obsessive are quite different. When we are obsessive, we lose our balance and we lose our way. Over-focus is as harmful as under-focus. Being obsessive is being overly focused to the point where we are no longer seeing clearly."

I was very interested and was mentally toying with the concept of balance when he said, "Yes. Part of trying easy involves balance. I will give you an example. There are folks who are so passionate about their dream that they over-train or overwork. They lose their focus because they are trying too hard. Achieving your dream means going the extra miles and doing what needs to be done and also, remembering to eat properly and get enough sleep. Take your job on Earth seriously, but not too seriously, and maintain a sense of concern and care for what others need. No one ever failed at life that made his or her life an act of kindness. Remember to keep your mind quiet enough each day so that you can hear what you are being told by the Creator. We need to ask for grace and discipline when we feel lost, unsure, or without hope, and when we are tired, we need to rest."

I was stuck on thinking about the importance of kindness and needed more time to process my thoughts; but he kept speaking and I didn't want to miss anything, so I forced myself to pay attention.

"Trying easy also means seeing yourself smiling, in your mind's eye, as you perform what is required of your sport, job, or appointed task. Put in the preparation time and then visualize winning. See yourself hitting the ball, scoring the shot, or getting the contract. See yourself trying easy and getting the job done because you are relaxed and prepared."

"Okay, Coach, I think I can do that, but you also told me that I have to remember to keep my mind quiet. How do I do that?"

"You learned how to do it. Meditate. Every day, take time to meditate so that you can listen to what you are being told. It is a great help for staying balanced. It will also guide you to understand how everything and everyone is connected in a dance that lasts until we die. Meditation will provide you with the focus and direction you need to make your dreams come true. That is why I asked you to sit with me at 5 AM and meditate ... to clear and open your mind ... to prepare for the day ahead."

"What did you mean about asking for grace? What is grace and who do I ask?"

"Grace is God's gift to humanity. It is inspiration. It is direction. It is discipline. Most of all, grace is an expression of love from the Creator. Did I answer your question?"

I answered, "I think so. I need to think about it!"

"City Bear, I am going to a give you another gift that can help you to make great progress toward your dream. **It is your Seventh Gift.**"

"I'm listening."

"On your way to your dream, if you would like to tap into a bottomless reservoir of wisdom and support, talk to your ancestors. Those who were here before you and have passed to the next plane want to assist you and are always trying to help. When you die, you go back to where you came from and become part of the Infinite Intelligence, the Creator. Your ancestors are connected to a source of information that is limitless. They have become one with the Creator, and yet they care about you, because their genetic composition—their human code, so to speak—is similar to yours. If they knew you and loved you when they were alive—that love never dies. In fact, it continues to grow as they watch you unfold in your earthly life. They want to help and protect you. They are here in another dimension, and they are always with you. They are part of you like the color of your eyes or hair. They want what is best for you, even when it seems that your life is not going the way you want. Remember, the oak tree that has survived many storms has roots very deep in the earth. The ordeals of our lives can increase our strength and rootedness or destroy us. How we cope with our trials defines our level of adequacy."

"Asking my ancestors for help is an interesting thought. I like the idea. My father died in 1994, and I think of him every day. Sometimes I can almost feel his presence when I talk to him. He was a great mechanic and I'm not. Whenever I have to do something that takes mechanical ability, I think of him and ask for his guidance. I believe that he's here and wants to help. I believe that there are others who have passed who also want to help … but I haven't asked."

"Why not?"

"I guess I didn't think of it."

"Now you can feel free to think of it! City Bear, **the Eighth Gift is a continuation of the Third Gift: Stop running from your problems and instead, embrace them lovingly, as you might hug a son or daughter.** You would learn very little that is important in your spiritual evolution without your problems. You need them like a student needs to take classes to learn. You need your problems, as well as problem people, for you to progress."

"I want to go back to the ancestor thing. How do I access my ancestors? Is there any special technique that I should know that can get me better reception—a clearer connection?"

I wondered if he might be annoyed because I didn't follow his train of thought and instead, asked for confirmation about a prior concept. He didn't seem to mind and answered, "When you go to a diner, how do you get a cup of coffee?"

"I ask the waitress."

"Do you always get your coffee right away?"

"No, sometimes she's busy and I have to wait."

"Remember in the Bible where it says, 'Ask and you shall receive?' Well, there is more to it than just asking. Sometimes you shall receive but maybe not right away, or maybe you do not receive because what you are asking for would not be good for you."

"Okay, let me see if I've got it. I ask for coffee and maybe I get it and maybe I don't, or I get it but by the time I do, I might not be drinking coffee or I might need something stronger."

"That is close enough for now. There is more for you to learn. Remember to talk to your ancestors. Ask people you loved and continue to love even though they have died, because love never dies. Love is the power that has created and orders the universe and everything in it. The Creator is pure love. I have used the masculine form when speaking about the Creator because we are used to it. The Creator does not need to be masculine or feminine, because pure love encompasses everything. He is speaking to us all the time through our ancestors and also through people who enter our lives.

He puts them there so that we can learn from them, and He speaks to us through them."

"What do you mean, He speaks to us through them? How does it happen?"

"People are telling us all the time what they need. Some need attention; others need money for lunch or dinner; some need advice; some need our time; some need to be told that you love them but do not approve of their behavior; and some need to feel that someone cares."

"How do I know? Most people don't tell you what they need."

"It is more than that! Most folks may not know what they need."

"If they don't know, how am I supposed to know?"

"My grasshopper friend, remember our exercises. Listen for what is said and also for what is *not said*. When you practice keeping your mind quiet as you go about your day, you will hear the words of those who have become part of your life and also sense what is in their heart, even if they are pretending. Remember the notes of the wood flute and the silence between the notes. That was lesson one, wasn't it?"

"Yeah."

"And there is more. The love we have in us for others is the most important part of us. The love we have for those who cannot do anything for us is the part of us that is divine. The more we practice kindness, the more we come in touch with the Creator's love within us, the more we see and hear, because we are not focused on our own music but rather, the music of others. The more we practice kindness toward others, who are not kind toward us, the more God's love flows through us and the more we become capable of making a difference, and the higher our vibration."

"What do you mean, the higher our vibration?"

"As our vibration increases, we move closer to the perfect vibration of the Creator."

I was deeply absorbed in thinking about the Creator's vibration when he said, "I mentioned it before, and I am saying it again because it is so important: sometimes love is saying no or saying something that needs to be said, but you do not want to say it. Sometimes it is facing those who dislike you and want to hurt you, and then taking action to prevent them from doing so. Sometimes love may seem harsh, firm, or demanding. Greatness in any discipline or endeavor never comes from a teacher who always tells us how wonderful we are, but rather from the teacher who demands our best and holds us to standards which we may believe are beyond our reach."

"This kindness thing is a big deal with you, isn't it?"

"It is everything. If people became kinder and more compassionate, there would be no wars, no starving people, and no crime. People would take care of each other, and the Earth would become paradise. Some people would also be made aware that their health and happiness depends on their thoughts and actions toward others; that they must change, if they want to be healthy and happy."

"The last part doesn't sound easy."

"Nothing worthwhile is. I want to say more to you about our ancestors. They have completed their earthly journey, and now they know what is important. They want to help us and spend their time trying to get through to us. The quieter your mind becomes, the more they can get through and give you what you need. Practicing the quieting of your mind is something that will have great benefits in your life as you move toward the realization of your dreams."

"Okay, let's say I work every day at quieting my mind. How will I know when the Creator or my ancestors are trying to contact me?"

"It is subtle—fainter than a whisper. Or perhaps a thought that makes sense—accompanied by a challenge to act. We always get the option to choose. City Bear, before I forget, on your way to your dream, remember to take out the garbage."

"You lost me there. Take out the garbage?"

"We all have an earthly job. We have to do those mundane

things that are part of daily life. We have to mow the lawn, shop for food, take the kids to school, and help with homework. All of us have to do those things that we do not want to do, like waiting in a bank line, sitting in traffic, putting up with a whiney family member or friend or someone at work whom we do not like. When I say take out the garbage, I mean everything that is part of our life process that is necessary but uninspiring. Most folks do not look forward to taking out the garbage; and if they do not, it will eventually stink."

"I'm on overload. I've got a lot to think about, and I'd like to take a walk by myself."

"Good! Walking is good. You are on your own today. Star and I will be away for the rest of the day and will not be back until late this evening. Your lunch and dinner are in the refrigerator. She left a note on the kitchen table about heating directions. Your snacks are on the counter next to the refrigerator."

I didn't think it was appropriate to ask where they were going. With all this time for myself, I asked, "Would you mind if I looked at the books in your library?"

Coach responded, "Mi casa es su casa!" and walked toward the back door. As he spoke, I could hear the full-bodied thump of the diesel engine in the Ford pickup and assumed Star was driving.

I needed some ice water, and when I opened the door of the refrigerator, I saw handwritten notes on top of two white ceramic containers designated Lunch and Dinner. Both notes had a smiley face on the bottom with Ms U written next to each.

Smiley faces and Ms U declarations are more representative of teenagers than adults, but I liked it.

The snacks were on small paper plates that had been covered in clear plastic wrap. Under the wrap, in black marker, on a white strip of paper, the snacks were identified: 10AM, 3PM, and 7PM. I opened the 10 AM package, poured a glass of ice water, and ate the four-inch piece of celery that was topped with chunky peanut butter. I was looking forward to seeing his library in the full light of day and quickly finished the snack.

Though the sun had lit the room, I put on the overhead lights to help me read the book titles. The largest section was on Social Science, Self-help, Healing, and Psychology. I recognized some of the names: Jampolsky, Ellis, Chopra, Borysenko, Williamson, Choquette, and Dyer. He also had a collection of books about Edgar Cayce and Paul Solomon.

I love reading, and this was paradise. I went back to the kitchen, made myself a cup of coffee, and brought it back to the library. I had taken a pile of books from the shelves and placed them on a table next to a plush easy chair in his living room—the kind that has a lever on the side and the front folds out for leg support. I always take notes when I'm reading, and I brought a notebook and pen with me. I was set—I had coffee, easy chair with leg adjustment, paper and pen, and lots of books, and me with no responsibilities. *This ain't bad.* "This isn't bad" just wouldn't have captured the moment.

I spent the day walking, reading, taking notes, and in between, enjoying Star's cooking. By the time I was ready for bed, I had compiled about fifteen pages of notes from the books of a half dozen authors. Coach and Star had not returned when I went to my room to write in my journal, and I wondered what was so important that they both had to be gone for so long. I figured it was none of my business, but I still thought about it. After a cool shower, I sat at the desk and began to make my entries.

Day Two

Today I received three more gifts, and I know the practice of each will lead me closer to the achievement of my mental, physical, spiritual, and financial goals.

When I'm with Coach, he makes me feel like I am the most important person in the world, and he focuses on what I have to say and seems more than willing to answer my questions. He is a very unusual man and his words and actions suggest he is dedicated to the mission outlined by his abbot. Though I have only been here two days, I know I have changed, but I'm not exactly sure how. I do know that I am thinking more about what I can do for others and less about myself. Today's gifts were:

Gift Six

In order to be able to "try easy," you have to be willing to do things on a regularly scheduled basis that most people will not do to develop the skills the sport or task requires.

Gift Seven

On the way to your dream, take time to talk on a daily basis with your ancestors. They want to help you and are connected to a source of information that is limitless.

Gift Eight

Stop running from your problems and instead, embrace them as you might lovingly hug a son or daughter.

Today I took two walks, one in the afternoon and another after dinner. I am amazed at what I see and hear that I would not have seen or heard before my training with Coach.

I kept Star's notes with the smiley faces and am thankful for her Ms U signature.

That's enough for today.

I closed the journal and got under the sheet and light cotton cover. I was mentally reviewing the events of the day and wondered again why Star and Coach had taken so long to return as I drifted toward sleep.

Chapter Seventeen

In the world I came from, there are too many people talking unnecessarily almost all the time.

The Benefits of Silence

The bells—it must be 4:30 AM. Meditation. Silence. When Coach arose from meditation, he said, "City Bear, in fifteen minutes, meet me on the sandy patch overlooking the wildflowers."

When I arrived, he was already doing his stretching exercises. I was wondering if I had offended him in some way or done something wrong, because the day before when he told me I was on my own for the day, he seemed distant.

Yesterday, during our exercise time, he spoke very little. At the beginning of the session, he said, "Do your best to copy the stretches and exercises I show you."

He motioned for me to sit and said, "It is important to stretch. Animals do it all the time. Did you ever see a lion or tiger after they get up from sleep? They stretch. They loosen up. They prepare for whatever it is they have to do that day or night. Most people forget that we are not far removed from the animal world. If we miss more than a few days of eating, our civilized behavior can change in ways difficult to imagine."

He had me thinking about the animals and their practice of stretching when I heard him say, "Now, you do it!"

I sat with the grace of an arthritic penguin and tried to imitate him. I did my best and was very happy that Star was not watching.

Next, he rolled from the sitting position to his stomach, with his hands in push-up position but pointing inward toward each other and straightened his arms, which pushed his shoulders upward. At the same time, he pressed his hips and legs into the sand and arched his head and neck back toward his feet.

"This is called the Cobra. It is very effective yoga posture and great for stretching the back. I have done it every day for as long as I can remember—now you try."

I finished the Cobra and watched him as he took a six-foot wooden pole, about two inches in diameter, and placed it behind his neck. His palms, facing upward, held the pole about six inches from each end. Then, standing straight, he began twisting slowly from side to side with the pole making almost a ninety-degree turn in each direction. I counted fifty twists.

"Your turn," he said.

I copied his movements and felt the pressure of the stick as it opened up my back. I could feel the muscles elongate and loosen. When I finished, my back was not as tight.

"That felt great!"

"Our bodies are very fancy machines. In fact, they are the only machines that have the capacity to repair themselves. In some ways, they remind me of diesel engines. Diesels are made to run. Most farmers and truckers have diesels because once they get started, it seems they can run forever. They just keep going. It is not uncommon for a farmer to have a diesel tractor for thirty or forty years. The worst thing you can do to a diesel is not to run it for a long period of time. It is the same with us. We need to move and run our engine, our body. Stretching helps the body get started. Like a glow plug helps to start a diesel."

I finished the twists and asked, "Is that it?"

"Almost. I will be right back."

He returned with what appeared to be a gray beach ball, and he sat on it with his feet on the ground. Then he extended his legs and rolled his back onto the ball. Slowly he rocked himself on his back, with his head arched toward the ground and his back arched over the ball.

While he was rocking back and forth, he said, "This also opens up the chest and increases spinal flexibility."

When he finished, I attempted to copy his movements, and immediately I noticed the ball was much thicker than a beach ball. It felt heavy and durable, with a strong rubber smell, like a car tire. This was no kiddy toy. I felt like it could easily handle the weight of an NFL lineman.

Slowly, I rocked back and forth, and after a minute or so, I heard him singing and watched him playing an air guitar. He was smiling and apparently getting a big kick out of his performance. Whatever it was that may have been bothering him yesterday seemed to have vanished.

He sang, "On the road again. Just can't wait to get on the road again. The life I love is making music with my friends, and I can't wait to get on the road again."

It was the first time I heard him use a contraction *can't*, and I said, "Coach, I thought I heard Willie on the sound system in your house when I first came here. Was I right?"

"Willie is the man! He is the poet of the workingman and he has had enough pain for three lifetimes, and yet he still smiles and brings joy to millions of people. Our government tried to ruin him, and he bounced back stronger than ever. He has made lots of mistakes in his life, as we all have. I am going to ask for his help in your mission. We will talk about that later in the week."

Whoa! He is going to ask him to help me. He is going to ask Willie Nelson to help me with my mission to help save Mother Earth. This is getting more bizarre by the day. Maybe by graduation, Willie and I will have become best buds and be writing songs together. This was immediately followed by my recognition that I was thinking like a lunatic.

He paused for a few seconds and said, "When I learned English, I was never taught contractions, because they are abbreviations of words, and my instructor, another monk from England, had never felt comfortable with them; however, singing *cannot wait to get on the road again* would sound like Japanese karaoke."

My thought about contractions had been answered without asking.

I finished stretching, and while in the process of getting up, watched Coach, with his mirrored blue sunglasses, repeating the lyrics and playing the air guitar. It was funny. I had never seen this side of him. I smiled and thought: *Willie would be flattered to know that the man, considered by some to be the world's greatest healer, sings his songs and plays the air guitar.*

We followed the stretching with a kettlebell routine that was a killer, and by the time we finished, I felt like my arms were no longer part of my body.

Kettlebells look like cannonballs with a handle and have been used for decades by Russian strongmen for conditioning and strength training. I followed his lead, and during the workout, he gave me the short course on kettlebell theory, as well as his thoughts about the most effective exercises.

After the kettlebell workout, Coach said, "During your stay, I am introducing you to a variety of stretching, aerobic, and strength-building exercises. You decide which work best for you and maybe you will find some additional practices that I have not shown you. It is very important that you stretch, build muscle strength, and improve your aerobic capacity. How you do it is up to you. You must work each of the three areas mentioned with regularity and intensity for the exercises to work. Be careful not to train the same muscle groups within forty-eight hours. Your body needs the rest to rebuild the muscle tissue that has been stressed by your workout."

Breakfast followed. The table was set and the food was ready when we got there, and still no Star. It was almost 7:00 AM when we finished. There was no conversation. I had hoped that the singing and air guitar performance had taken his mind off whatever it was that seemed to be bothering him yesterday. The silence was starting to bother me when he said, "You did not do anything wrong yesterday or today. I am not angry with you. I want you to realize that silence is acceptable. Constant chatter is not healthy."

I felt better, but I hadn't thought I talked all that much.

He then asked, "Are you ready for our morning stroll?"

Before I could answer, he said, "Meet me in thirty minutes at the back of the house, and wear your hiking boots and a hat."

I wondered what a "stroll" meant to him and then pictured myself wearing only what he told me—a hat and hiking boots. I laughed and thought: *that picture would scare the children, if any were around.*

When I arrived, he tossed a canteen to me, which I assumed was filled with water, and said, "You are going to need this!"

I figured he just answered my question about the stroll. I wondered if I'd survive.

"Apaches used to run a hundred or more miles in a day and think nothing of it!"

"I'm Irish and German, with a touch of Norwegian. That will usually get me to the nearest bar or delicatessen. So, how far do you plan to go?"

"Not too far!"

I wondered what not too far meant to him, and I was hoping that he was anything but Apache. *Perhaps a sedentary tribe that made baskets or jewelry would be nice.*

We walked into the desert at a pace that caused me to half jog. This was not a stroll. This was boot camp, and after about a half hour, he said, "You need to drink some water. We are halfway there, and we will rest for a few minutes before we continue."

I started to say something about the desert when he interrupted and said, "Be silent! You talk too much. Instead of talking, pay attention to what is going on around you."

I hadn't said a word since we left the house and thought that he was being overly authoritative with his command not to speak. I sipped three or four mouthfuls from the canteen and repressed any urge I had for conversation. On the return trip, I seemed to be focused less on my thoughts and more on my environment. By the time we arrived at the ranch, I had noticed sights, sounds, and smells that I'd missed on the way out. I saw a yellow-headed woodpecker poking his head out of a cactus. There was a rotten meat smell when we passed a clump of sage. I remembered thinking; *maybe an animal had died and the scavengers hadn't finished the job of picking the bones clean.* There was the sound of an unidentified bird chirping in a thick patch of prickly pear cactus. I saw animal tracks near the prickly pear and wanted to ask Coach what he thought they were, but decided against it.

By the time we got back to the ranch, I felt very comfortable with the silence: *in the world I came from, there are too many people talking unnecessarily almost all the time.*

As he was opening the back gate, he turned to me and said, "You just walked eight miles in a little over two hours. Not bad for a city bear! Think about what you learned today. Write it down in your journal so that you will not forget it. Lunch will be at noon, and I suggest you begin to work on your plan to inspire others by becoming the person you always wanted to be … with no pretending."

"What do you mean? You keep saying with no pretending."

Coach stopped walking, faced me, and said, **"Your Ninth Gift is: Starting today, when you return to your room, begin seeing yourself as the person you always wanted to be, and capture that person in your journal.** See him and become him through daily practice."

I was thinking that this would not be an easy task when he continued, "Remember my admonition. Your life, even if you live to be very old, is very short. Do not waste your life!"

"Coach, I'll do what you're asking, but how do I know who I am with no pretending?"

I could sense he was getting impatient with me when he continued, "When you get back to your room, you will begin to write your plan to change the world. You will begin this plan by writing your plan for your life. I am asking you to dream and to make your dream come true for the purpose of making your life count. In order to change the world, you must start with yourself. Start by writing down what you can do to become your best self mentally, physically, spiritually, financially, and most of all, in your relationships with your family, friends, co-workers, and community."

I had more questions but again decided not to ask.

While Coach looked refreshed, I looked whipped. He looked as if he had just stepped out of an invigorating shower, toweled off, and put on fresh clothes. Before I did anything, I wanted a long drink of ice-cold water and a trip to the shower.

Star was setting the table for lunch when I arrived at the courtyard about five minutes early. I decided to think Bond, James Bond, the coolest man who ever lived, and I attempted to make a really suave entrance. She must have heard me coming, because she turned, faced me, and flashed her gazillion-dollar smile. I was trying to be so cool, my feet got tangled up and I tripped. Not a little stumble that could easily be corrected, but rather an ass-over-teakettle trip that had me spread out like a cornered fugitive on the TV show *Cops*. I had shorts on and skinned my knee. It started to bleed. Not arterial blood, just a trickle.

Her smile vanished and she looked concerned. I felt like Shamu flopping around on the concrete in the Sea World aquarium; nevertheless, I retained my cool and said, "That smile of yours blinded me, and I couldn't see where I was going." In spite of it all, my comeback made me feel very Bondish, even if I didn't appear that way.

"You are a very loveable City Bear! Do you know that?"

"I'm sorry, I didn't hear you."

She repeated what she said, and I said, "I really heard you the first time, but I liked it so much, I wanted to hear it again."

She shook her head and asked, "Is your knee okay? I will get some cold water to rinse the cut and put some iodine on it!"

I insisted that it was nothing and that she continue getting lunch. I was thanking her for her concern when Coach arrived.

Again we had a thick soup with lots of vegetables and today some pieces of grilled chicken. She brought a frosty pitcher of lemonade with three tall glasses and placed one at each setting.

Star joined us for lunch, and we talked about the walk in the desert. Coach mentioned that we had walked about eight miles, and she seemed impressed. I acted like I did it all the time, and she said during our conversation, "That is quite a walk in this heat!"

I could feel myself blushing, and I felt proud. I asked her about her trip yesterday; she said that she had been visiting some friends and Coach picked her up on his way home. She said that he had some business concerns that had taken his attention and kept him in town until late in the evening.

Today, she had on a blue sundress with white embroidery and matching moccasins. I mentioned that the dress was very pretty, and she said she made it herself and enjoyed sewing. She shared that she made most of her clothes.

Wow! I never met someone who made her own clothes.

The lunch discussion ended, and she began to clean up. I asked if I could help, but she insisted that I couldn't because I was a guest.

I spent the afternoon by myself. I wrote in my journal, read, and walked by the wildflowers, hoping that she would see me and come out to chat. I was coming back to the house when I saw her car turning onto the road and heading west. I felt a sense of loss, like a kid at camp who misses his family. When I went to dinner, there was a note:

City Bear, Star and I have to meet again with some folks about our problems with the deed. Dinner is in the refrigerator and just needs to be warmed up. See you tomorrow!

There were snacks on the counter, and the note was signed Coach. I wondered why Star didn't write the note and thought about the smiley faces I had placed in my wallet.

Day 3

That night, before I retired, I wrote five pages that were related to my Ninth Gift. Page one listed what I wanted to look like physically; page two described how I wanted to improve myself mentally; page three depicted what I wanted to realize in my spiritual evolution; page four listed my financial goals; and page five the goals for my relationships with family, friends, co-workers, and community.

I fell asleep playing the audiotape in my mind, over and over, listening to her say, "You are a very loveable City Bear!"

Chapter Eighteen

Forgiveness does not mean being a doormat others can wipe their feet on.

To Live is to Suffer

The routine for day four was the same as the first three days: bells, meditation, exercise, and breakfast. Crispy brown French toast and lean turkey sausage patties were presented on a silver serving dish, accompanied by a mound of blueberries and again, six almonds, presented in the shape of a circle. A steaming bowl of oatmeal with cinnamon and raisins added to the feast, and the smell of hot coffee wafted from the carafe on the table.

Star poured tea for Coach and smiled at me before she asked if she could pour my coffee. I smiled back and nodded, as I reminded myself of my skinned knee and yesterday's acrobatics. I didn't want to say or do something embarrassing again. She had breakfast with us and spoke about her recent visit with her father. I listened, smiled, and nodded appropriately, as I reminded myself that she could read my thoughts. I was hoping Coach might have to go on an emergency trip to South America, or maybe the Arctic.

Coach then said, "Meet me on the sandy patch overlooking the wildflowers in fifteen minutes," which interrupted my thoughts.

Star took my plate and asked me to hand her the silverware;

then asked if I would like another cup of coffee. Coach had left the table, and I thought it would be best to get ready for my next lesson. I know she knew I wanted to stay and talk, and when she took away the dishes; she looked at me and said, "We will have time," and disappeared into the kitchen.

My mind was racing. Yesterday she had called me a loveable City Bear. Today she said, "We will have time!" I was Jell-O. The last time I felt like this, I was going to the senior prom and my date and I were in the back of my buddy's Chevy convertible.

I got it together and was a few minutes early for our meeting. He was doing some lunges with a kettlebell when I arrived, and after he finished the set he said, "Fundamentals. More fundamentals. Today I am not going to add to your gifts, but will provide you with some additional fundamentals. After today, we only have two days left, and you will be driving back on Sunday morning. We still have a substantial amount of work to do."

The thought of having only two days left made me anxious. I didn't feel anywhere close to being ready for graduation and my mission.

He began, "Today's fundamentals include: always start your days the night before by writing down what you plan to accomplish the next day. List the time you will get out of bed and start your day. I suggest you arise at 4:30 AM. I realize that you may not always be able to arise at that time. There is a great deal to do and not enough time to do it all. Your time is precious. Do not waste it."

I remembered hearing him say, during one of our seated meditations, "Your life, even if it is very long, is very short. Do not waste your life." This variation carried the same message and I said, "That's awfully early, Coach."

"Then do not do it. Most people would not, and think it was asking too much. Most folks would not understand and that is okay. They do not have to do what you have been chosen to do. Although, maybe I should not say that, because in time, you will be asking some of them who are like-minded and want to make a difference to do the same."

"Is this mandatory? What happens if I don't get up and sleep until 8 or 9:00?"

"You will be scalped and your hair hung from my teepee."

"You're joking."

"Maybe Theophane did make a mistake? Where is your sense of humor? Of course I am joking. I do not have a teepee. I live in a house!"

"Very funny, Coach. But suppose I don't get up?"

"Then you will get less done and help less people. It is entirely up to you. It is your life. You can do more, if you use your time wisely.

"The benefit of writing down what you plan to accomplish the next day is that you have a road map of what you plan to do and when you plan to do it. I suggest after you write down the plan for the following day that you see the day unfolding in your mind's eye; see the day as if you are watching a movie, and feel elated about each activity as you complete it. Knowing you are on your way to making your dreams come true. Most important is seeing yourself getting out of bed when most folks are not up for another two hours. I realize some people get up earlier than 6:30, but most do not."

I'm not crazy about getting up that early.

"The value of the 4:30 approach is that during the time from 4:30 to 6:30, when most people are sleeping, you will have accomplished at least two solid hours of focused work. This is the time to write, to exercise, to think and plan, to focus on your dreams and set into action those thoughts that will guide you on your way. The key is starting the night before and writing a detailed plan of what you want to accomplish the following day—with the time you will arise clearly marked on your plan."

"How can I get up that early without being exhausted during the day?"

"City Bear, you are an intelligent man. What do you think the answer to your question is?"

"Go to bed earlier."

"There is hope! I was beginning to worry. By all means, go to bed early. Is there anything really important going on after 9:00?"

"Some people would say so. Movies. Talking with friends. Sport games. Letterman or Leno. Reading. Most people use the hours after 9:00 to unwind."

"Why do they need to unwind?"

"Stress. Living is stressful, Coach. Not everyone lives in the middle of nowhere, grows wildflowers, and has a live-in niece to help with the housework. People have stress at work and in their personal lives. Life isn't easy."

"I see you have evaluated what my life is like, and after your review, determined that I am not faced with stressful situations or difficult people."

"I'm not trying to say that you don't have any stress, but you were a monk. You don't have a wife, kids, bills, or in my case, the problems of a job. I'm not sure you do know what stress is about."

"City Bear, no one escapes. I have had problems with my eyes since I was a child when I was injured in that explosion. I am concerned that someday I will not be able to see. I was very close to an older monk, who is now very sick, and I think of him often. He was like a second father to me. Star did not tell you, but there are people who want to take my home away. Though I purchased the land with all the proper paperwork and legal fees, there is a group of very powerful people who want to take it because someone told them about the underground spring."

"I'll bet they're white men who want to take your land."

"Wrong! They are brother Indians who have forgotten who they are."

"Wow! I'm surprised."

"You are like a lot of white people who have a romantic idea of

Indians. They are just like everyone else. There are good people and bad people in all races, and lots of folks in between."

"I guess that was pretty naive of me."

He didn't respond.

"They want the water. Their lawsuit is in the courts now, and the people who want the water know many of the local politicians, and I do not. When I have been away during the day, I have had to meet with lawyers, tribal leaders, and government agency people about keeping my land. It has been costly in both time and money, and I do not know what I will do if my home is taken away."

What a bummer. He bought the land legally, spent two years getting the house and land in shape, begins his work on his mission, and then has to worry about his home being taken away. What makes it even worse is that the perpetrators are brother Indians.

"City Bear, in some measure, I do not know who I am. That is why I am here: to find my father's people and learn if I have any living relatives. My family has always been the monks I lived with, and I remember very little of my mother or father. As you know, I have been chosen by my abbot to play a major role in healing a very sick planet. If I fail, Mother Earth will not heal for thousands of years and many people will perish. What I am saying is very real. The signs are all there. Do you still feel I do not know about stress?"

"I'm sorry about that. If you don't mind me asking, how do you cope with the problems you mentioned?"

"That is what Buddhism is about. To live is to suffer. It is how we address our suffering that determines the quality of our lives. Suffering is the result of ignorance, and ignorance is belief in a truly existing self and the solidity of phenomena. When we understand that so much of what we perceive as real is an illusion; that all life is transient; and the only certainty is that everything will change, we move toward a sense of inner calm. A calm that is based on knowledge of what is, and not what we *think* is. Also, there is consolation in knowing that we do not know what is good or bad for us. Remember, what seems to be bad may be good, and the opposite, as you have learned, also holds true—what seems to be good may be bad."

I was taking it all in and telling myself to make certain I wrote about our conversation in my journal that night. He paused for a few seconds, took a deep breath, and continued, "You are here to begin the process of acquiring knowledge, and as you do so you will need less time to unwind, because, in essence, the world will not be able to wind you. Arising at 4:30 will not be difficult and, in time, it will become joyful."

Joyful? Getting up in the middle of the night can be joyful? "Trust me," he responded without my saying a word.

"Isn't that what the spider said to the fly?"

"I am not a spider, and you are not a fly. I want to get back to our lesson."

"Okay, Coach, I'm listening."

"At the end of the day, review your plan, write what happened, and develop the plan for the next day. You will not always achieve what you plan, but you will get far more done than if you never had a plan. In looking at why your plan did or did not work each day, you will gain valuable information related to obstacles that are keeping you from completing important activities."

"Should I write down the reason something was not completed or just that I didn't finish it?"

"The reason, as well as what was not completed. By following this procedure, you will discover behavioral patterns you may not currently understand. When you prepare your plan for the following day, there are a few thoughts you might want to keep in mind. Many of these thoughts are related to information we have discussed. For example, do not plan to get up at 4:30 if you went to bed at midnight. It will not work. Remember, you need to get enough sleep to be effective, and seven and a half to eight hours is usually a minimum. Also, make sure your plan includes eating healthfully, drinking enough water, as well as proper exercise, meditation, and balance. Opportunities for practicing kindness will come about naturally, and be careful of your speech. Avoid speaking harshly or negatively about others, and if you cannot say something positive, it is better that you do not speak."

"What if someone is just plain no good and a really rotten person? Why shouldn't I say it?"

"Because it disturbs your serenity. The universe knows when someone is not living by its laws and always takes action, though possibly not in the timeframe we want. You do not need to do anything to bring about justice. Why waste your energy and breath on someone who does not deserve it? Save your time and energy for what is important."

I wondered about O.J. Simpson and how many people believed that he got away with murdering two people, and recently, it appears his arrest may put him in jail for a long time. Sometimes, evil people seem to get away with terrible deeds, and Coach's words echoed in my mind: "Not in the timeframe we want."

"You can learn from bad people, because they teach you what not to do, and you should thank them in your heart for being your teacher. They are teaching you by example. Why should you speak unfavorably about your teacher?"

"Coach, you want me to thank the people who are trying to hurt me?"

"More than that! I want you to forgive them and pray for them."

"You've got to be kidding."

"Would you feel better watching them suffer? Would that make you feel better?"

"No, I just want them to get what they deserve."

"I see. You have never done anything someone else could perceive as being nasty, mean, or uncaring?"

"I guess I have."

"You guess?"

"Okay! I know I have."

"So, unless you forgive others, you will not be forgiven. Have you heard that?"

"I think so."

"In your prayer, the Our Father, it is very clear. It asks God the Father to forgive us our trespasses, as we forgive those who trespass against us. That means if we forgive, we are forgiven. Part of being human includes making mistakes. Judging is so easy to do, and yet if we were being judged, we would want to be treated fairly, and in judging can we ever treat anyone fairly without knowing all the facts?"

I was listening as intently as I could and kept reminding myself to remember what he said so I could write it in my journal.

"Many of our judgments are based on incomplete knowledge. Often, we believe we know enough to make fair decisions, and we do not. Many times we make decisions about people based on illusions or false assumptions. We take the puzzle pieces given us and construct a picture that is sometimes the opposite of the true picture. Then we feel satisfied that we have been fair and just, while in fact, our picture is a reflection of our ignorance."

This is good stuff! How many times have juries found the defendant to be guilty when he or she was not? How many times have I made a mistake about someone's intentions? How many times have I heard something that later I find was half the real story; that the true story was not what was presented to me?

I knew I was changing and the change was subtle. I felt like a kid learning to ride a bike, and each day he practiced, he got a little better at it. Coach had been silent; I believe he knew I was trying to take in as much of what he said as possible, and knew I needed a few seconds for the information to percolate.

"Opportunities for kindness are all around us every day. As I mentioned yesterday, kindness also means setting limits for others and ourselves, and sometimes saying no to others and ourselves."

"So it could be kind of me to tell someone something they don't want to hear, even if it hurts their feelings?"

"Choose your words carefully and make certain whatever is said is offered with love and not because you are angry or want to get even. If you cannot take the time to choose your words carefully and you cannot speak with love in your heart, it is better you do not say anything."

"That's not easy." I stated.

"Where is it written that it is supposed to be? I want to get back to your daily plan. Make sure you read it as soon as you arise, and then three or four times during the day—after breakfast, lunch, and dinner. Before you go to bed read it again and evaluate your progress before you write your plan for the next day. Let the knowledge you gained today help you with your plan for tomorrow."

"This planning thing is a really big deal with you?"

"Yes!"

That was it—I needed to know more and asked, "Why? Why is it such a big deal?"

"Because it will determine the quality of your life. It will help you to be more aware of the minutes, the hours, and the days. None of us have forever, and the time we are given is our treasure. It is a treasure we can squander or use to enhance our own life and the lives of others. In your case, you have been given an opportunity to assist in the healing of the world, and that is a very rare honor. First, you must learn to heal yourself and using your time wisely is part of your life curriculum, and part of your healing."

"Coach, you've mentioned healing the world a few times, and I still don't get it. I'm one person, and I know, as you said, I can influence others, but healing the world seems overwhelming."

"Good! Maybe your fear will help you to listen better, pay attention, and learn quickly. Being overwhelmed is good. It means you realize you must change and grow if you are able to accomplish what needs to be done. When you read your plan for the next day the night before, and when you read it after arising, take a minute and see yourself doing whatever it is that you have written to do. See it happening, and when it is accomplished during the day, smile and feel reassured with the knowledge that you are moving forward toward your goals or dreams. You will have a sense of fulfillment that will be encouraging for you and contagious for others. People will want to know how you do it. How you seem to get lots of things done in an easy, relaxed manner. Sure, sometimes you will have to rush, we all do—let it be the exception rather than the rule and let yourself feel calm, peaceful and in charge of your life as you move closer and closer to where you want to be or what you want to achieve."

"Coach, I don't mean to be pushy, but I'm more than a little confused about this healing the world stuff, and your answers have not been real direct."

"You are right"

"Is that it? You are right!"

"When a seed is planted in the fall, do we expect a flower in the winter?"

"Coach, your answer sounds like a reading from a fortune cookie."

"What is a fortune cookie?"

"You don't know?"

He shook his head, indicating that fortune cookies were new to him.

"It's a thin, hollow cookie you get in Chinese restaurants, usually after dinner. It has a little piece of paper inside that has a wise saying, like a proverb, printed on it."

"Good. Maybe you will think of my answer as a wise saying," he said.

Coach, at times, was inscrutable, and I reminded myself that living with uncertainty is okay. I was learning that everything is uncertain anyway, so why worry about it? He was having an effect on my thinking, and I suspect that recognition would please him.

"It helps to get your mind and body functioning in the morning if, upon arising, you brush your teeth, wash your face, and have a cup of strong coffee or tea. While you put on the water for your hot drink, use the three or four minutes to stretch. Some basic yoga is great. Use the positions I taught you. After the water boils, get your drink and come back and finish. Your stretching should not take more than ten minutes, and it will do wonderful things for you. It will prepare your body for the day and help awaken your senses and get your mind ready for work. Take your coffee or tea with you when you begin your writing, exercising, reading, or planning. By 4:45 AM, you will be at work, and as I mentioned earlier, get more done before 6:00 or 7:00 AM than many folks will get done all day. You will start your day with a feeling of accomplishment. Because success breeds success, you have a better chance of keeping the success orientation moving throughout the day."

"Coach, I'll try, but that's awfully early." I had complained twice and wondered if he would be angry.

"Do not try. If you are going to try, do not bother at all. Do it and stop whining! Do you know that you whine, sometimes like a baby?"

"No. No one ever told me that."

"Good. Then I will be the first. As I am talking to you, I am remembering things you need to know, and one of them is this: I suggest you do not eat anything when you get up, but rather wait until you finish your first exercise period of the day at 6:30 or 7:00. If you eat in the morning, the blood goes to your stomach and not your brain. You need the blood in your brain to function most efficiently. So, after you complete your workout and shower, then have breakfast."

"Do you have any recommendations for breakfast? What do you suggest I eat?"

"A healthy cereal or oatmeal is good. Some fruit—a few almonds or raisins. Some protein—cottage cheese, eggs, turkey bacon, sausage, or hard cheese. Some coffee or tea. A glass of water is important. Any of the breakfasts that you have had here would be fine. Remember what I told you about eating less as the day progresses. Eat less for lunch than you ate for breakfast and less for dinner than you ate at lunch. In between meals and after dinner, before you retire for the evening, remember to snack. The snack will keep your blood sugar from getting too low, which causes hunger and fatigue. Your breakfast should be the main meal of the day, because you need the energy for the day's activities."

He spoke about this before, so it must be very important to him: eating more at breakfast than lunch or dinner. The larger breakfast would provide needed energy. As the day progresses, we generally need less and less energy as our bodies prepare for sleep. I liked the idea of small snacks and thought that eating less for lunch and dinner might help to control my weight.

"Coach, I noticed at breakfast each of us has a plate with six almonds. How come?"

"Edgar Cayce, the famous healer, believed that eating six almonds a day would prevent cancer. Cayce was a medical intuitive in the 1930s, and today, scientists are finding many of his remedies to be highly effective. From what I have read, he was a kind and compassionate man."

Interesting!

"Make sure you keep your portions small. That is important. Small portions will keep you from being hungry and help you lose weight. I know I have mentioned this before, but it needs to be repeated and practiced. During the day, see yourself taking care of your primary concerns."

"What does that mean?" I asked.

"Have you eaten properly? Did you get enough rest? If not, and you can, take a nap. If you cannot, try to find a quiet place and mediate for ten minutes. Did you exercise today? Make sure the exercise includes stretching, as well as aerobic and anaerobic exercise. Have you practiced frugality and generosity? By frugality, I mean before you spend money or put something on a credit card, did you ask yourself if you really need whatever it is? Can you make it or purchase it where it would be less costly? By generosity, I mean what have you done for someone else today? Have you given someone your time and attention, and in return cannot offer you anything? Have you helped someone who needs your assistance when you do not feel like it? At the end of the day, list where you were able to practice frugality and generosity—the less you need to be happy, the easier it is to be happy."

"What does practicing frugality have to do with changing the world? I understand about generosity, but frugality, what difference does it make?"

"When you are frugal, you practice doing with less or paying less. Having less releases you from possessions that are not yours anyway; they are only on loan. When you die, they will go to someone else. Paying less or doing with less also allows you to keep more of your money for things you really need, and because you have what you need, you do not feel desperate because of a lack of money."

"The fancy department stores won't get rich from you."

"I cannot argue with that. Also, while you list your areas of frugality and generosity, it is also a good time to focus on forgiveness. We spoke about that a few minutes ago. Think about when, during the day, you attempted to forgive someone who slighted you in some way, or maybe offended you. Turning the other cheek does not mean you can hit me on one cheek and I will turn the other so you can hit me again. Rather, I forgive what you did to my cheek and I will turn the other, if I think it was a mistake. I will also protect myself if you attempt to do it again, and this time you may get hurt. You may not have open season on both cheeks. Forgiveness does not mean being a doormat others can wipe their feet on. It means giving folks a chance but not a free ticket to hurt or insult you as they please."

"So it is okay to fight back?"

"It is not only okay, it is highly recommended. Being kind does not mean letting folks take advantage of you. It means giving folks the benefit of the doubt and being vigilant to protect yourself. Sometimes we have to protect ourselves with words and sometimes we need actions. Bullies love to abuse others; sometimes they do it with words and other times they do it physically. Part of learning to be a quality person is learning how to defend yourself and your loved ones, if they, or you, are being bullied. By giving the benefit of the doubt, maybe the first injury—emotional or physical—was an accident or inadvertent. When you turn the other cheek, watch for the action that suggests something else is coming, and if need be, protect yourself."

I was intrigued by his suggestions. Here was a holy man who, like Christ in the temple when he threw out the moneylenders, advised taking appropriate and protective action. I liked that!

"Some folks will only respect us if we react in a manner that very clearly states, 'I will not allow others, or myself, to be bullied.' Turning the other cheek to a bully is inviting disaster."

"Is there anything I can do to prepare myself for coping with bullies?"

"Learning the verbal and physical skills necessary to stand up for yourself helps. By the way, that doesn't mean we can win with all bullies because sometimes we do not have the verbal or physical skills to do so. It does mean making the bully think twice about picking on us. Bullies are cowards and usually pick on folks they know they can take advantage of, and when that person retaliates in some way and causes them pain, they are less likely to do it again. Sometimes we need the legal system, sometimes we need a friend to help us, and sometimes we need to confront the bully directly and let him or her know in whatever way appropriate that the season for picking on us is closed. We will not allow it and, if they continue their unacceptable behavior, it will not be in their best interest. There is a saying in Chinese that when translated means: 'Only the strong can afford to be gentle.' As you grow in your ability to effectively cope with bullies, you will become more gentle and more confident."

"Are you saying that taking on bullies is necessary in my work to heal the world?"

"Without question! The world got the way it is because too many people let bad things happen and did not do anything about it. I have always thought that the greatest sins of mankind are not sins of commission; but rather, omission where we failed to act and others were hurt because of it. Maybe the easiest way to answer your question is to return to the golden rule: treat others, as you would want to be treated. If you were being hurt, or harmed, at what point would you want someone to assist you?"

My mind was full of thoughts and questions when I heard him say, "That is enough for today." He walked into the house, and a few minutes later, I heard his truck drive away. He and Star once again were not around for lunch or dinner; and now I understood why. I surmised they had to spend time preparing their case for the land dispute lawsuit. The meals and directions for heating were left for me in the refrigerator.

I spent a good part of the day in his living room, reading and writing, and later, wandering about in the desert. I was beginning to feel comfortable with the silence, as well as being alone, and I knew I had a lot to write in my journal, even though much of what I was taught was not presented as a gift—and I wondered why. I wondered what new knowledge he considered a gift and why I had not been told that any of his thoughts or directions today—were gifts.

After dinner, I spent some time walking near the wildflowers and later reading and note-taking. I decided to get to my journal before I became too tired to do it justice.

I went to my room, turned on the longhorn light, sat down, and opened the journal to the next blank page.

Day 4

I haven't seen much of Star today. I think I know what is taking so much of their time away from the ranch. I spent the better part of the morning with Coach, and though our conversation gave me a great deal to think about, none of his thoughts or suggestions were presented as gifts, and I'm not sure why. He did say that I would be presented with what he defined as "more fundamentals."

The fundamentals I learned today were: always start your days the night before by writing down what you plan to accomplish the next day, and list the time you will get out of bed to start your day. He suggested I arise at 4:30 AM.

I made some notes about this morning's conversation while reading in the library. The thoughts I remember are as follows:

- To live is to suffer. It is how we address our suffering that determines the quality of our lives.
- When I change my perceptions, the world will not be able to wind me.
- Write my plan for the following day before I go to bed and review what happened during the day that helped or hindered the completion of today's plan.
- Speaking "bad" about people is a waste of energy, even if they deserve it.
- Forgive and pray for those who hurt me. For me to be forgiven, I have to forgive.
- Many of our judgments are based on incomplete information.
- Opportunities for the expression of our kindness are around us every day.
- Be careful of criticism. If you can't take the time to choose your words carefully and you can't speak with love in your heart, it's better you remain silent.
- Learning to use time wisely will enhance the quality of my life.
- My largest meal should be breakfast, lunch smaller, and dinner the smallest.
- Make sure to eat three healthy snacks every day.
- Practice frugality and generosity.

- The less I need to be happy, the easier it is to be happy.
- In order to complete my mission, I will have to effectively deal with bullies.

The above poured out onto the paper like water out of a pitcher. *This is interesting!* Though there were no specific gifts, I had identified important concepts he taught me and remembered them without trying. If my intuition was correct, he wanted me to begin to identify important information without him giving his imprimatur. I wondered if I was correct or the victim of my own illusion.

I closed the journal, turned off the light, and got in bed, but I couldn't turn off my mind. So much had happened. I had reprocessed much of what he said, and I was wondering about their success—or lack thereof—with the lawyers, tribal leaders, and politicians when my mind jumped to Star's departing words: "Don't worry. We will have time."

While musing about her comment, I fell into a deep sleep.

Chapter Nineteen

It is in the changing of the now that defines who you are and who you will be.

The Joy is in the Now

I was awake before the bells and heard Star's footsteps as she walked down the hallway. When she tapped the bells, I thought about having only one day left before I returned home.

I was looking forward to today's meditation, as well as the gift or gifts for the day. As soon as I was seated, Coach got up without making a sound and struck a large bronze gong, the size of a city stop sign, with a heavy wooden felt-tipped drumstick and proclaimed sternly: "Your life, even if it is very long, is very short. Do not waste your life!"

He had announced this caveat before, and I know it affected me, because sometimes, in the quiet of the day or evening, when alone, his words would play back in my mind, as if someone had turned on a tape recorder.

After the gong and his statement, we spent the next twenty to thirty minutes in silence. At the end of the meditation, he usually stood up and left. I knew that I was expected to meet with him for our morning exercises and had followed this routine since the second day.

Today, at the end of our session, he asked me to remain seated, take a deep breath, and inhale the scent of the burning sage and said, "Let the sage enter every cell of your body and purify you. You will need to prepare yourself for the tasks that await you. Breathe, think of the sage cleaning your mind and body from the inside out, and visualize all the negative or unhealthy thoughts and toxins in your body floating through the tips of your fingers to the tips of the incense, where they are burned and destroyed."

I followed his directive and inhaled the sage. I felt its power washing all my internal organs and the residue burned by the incense. It seemed like only a minute or two before he stood up and walked away. I stayed for an extra few minutes; the feeling was so comforting and peaceful, I didn't want it to end so quickly.

Our morning exercises, as usual, included yoga, calisthenics, and kettlebells. Today he added some kettlebell swings and lifts that were new. He also increased the intensity and duration of the workout and performed the exercises with a kettlebell that was almost double the size of the one I used. He told me my form for the exercises had improved, and he advised me to keep a record of the repetitions and weight used for each exercise. The idea was to slowly increase the repetitions and weight. At the end of the workout, I felt limber, strong, and ready for a shower.

I was the first at breakfast and seated when Star came to the table with a pot of tea, a carafe of coffee, a pitcher of ice water, cream, sugar, three cups, and three glasses.

The same clean, linen-like smell lightly permeated the air around her, and today she was wearing form-fitting jeans and a white cotton blouse with yellow and blue butterflies. The butterflies were made from tiny colored beads sewn onto the fabric. She wore light brown cowboy boots, and her hair was pulled back into a ponytail tied with a beaded kerchief with the same butterfly pattern.

"I hope that third cup means you'll be joining us?"

"Yes," she answered, "but first I have to get the rest of the breakfast."

She returned with a tray that held three bowls of oatmeal, as well as a large serving dish with country sausage, and scrambled eggs with peppers, cheese, and onions. The tray also held a bowl with sliced bananas, strawberries, and peaches, as well as the miniature plates for the almonds. I could smell the bread before it arrived. It was homemade, heavy, marbled, and still hot. It smelled like pumpernickel.

"Do you know this is my favorite breakfast?"

"By now, you shouldn't have to ask that question."

No matter how many times she demonstrated her talent, I forgot Coach had taught her to read minds. I suspect I didn't want to admit it to myself because it made me too vulnerable.

Before I could respond, she said, "I wanted to make something special for you. We don't have much time left, and I was hoping maybe this afternoon, after lunch, we could go for a walk."

I tried to restrain my exuberance and said, "I guess I can fit in a walk."

She knew what I was feeling, and when she looked at me, we both laughed. I was as transparent as a squeaky-clean window, and I had given up any attempt at being suave. I am not suave, cool, sophisticated, or urbane, and I had decided to be just me.

As if on cue, Coach entered the courtyard and sat down. Star was seated, and he said, "Star, our City Bear, is progressing very nicely with the kettlebells and exercises."

He turned to me and said, "I expect that by following the exercise routine I have shown you, as well as the dietary suggestions, in six months you will not look like the same person. I expect you will lose about forty pounds and have the energy of a thirty-year-old."

"Thanks! I'm glad you are happy with my progress."

Star said, "You know you are expected to return here in six months to discuss your mission progress, and I am confident that the new City Bear will be very pleased with his progress. In order to help the people who need you, you must make the necessary adjustments. You must lead by example, and I believe you will do it. "

"I didn't know I would be expected to return in six months."

Coach never addressed my concern about the six-month return schedule and instead said, "Tomorrow you will be given the details of your mission after the initiation ceremony. There is so little time; we have to make progress as quickly as possible."

"Initiation? Mission? Can we talk about this?"

"Relax. Enjoy the breakfast. You will learn everything you need to know in the time you need to know it!"

Star broke the moment of silence that followed by saying, "City Bear and I are going for a walk this afternoon, and I'm sure our conversation will help with his questions."

When he got up to leave, he said to me, "Meet me at the sandy patch in fifteen minutes. I have something very important to talk to you about."

He was friendly but stern, and it made me nervous. I cleaned up my room, and when I arrived, he was already seated.

As usual, he sat overlooking the wildflowers and motioned for me to sit next to him.

He began, "We have covered many important thoughts. As I instructed you yesterday, I want you to see yourself being whoever you have always wanted to be. You will see yourself as looking, acting, and feeling like that person. You will begin seeing yourself handle disappointment, difficulty, and rejection, as well as how you approach others and how you cope with everyday difficulties in a positive, relaxed, and joyful manner. Your days of being a scared rabbit are over. You will face all of your adversities and enemies with a sense of thankfulness, because you accept that they have been given to you as course material to improve your life and make you a sharper instrument for the work of the Creator.

"Joyful? I'm going to cope with problems in a joyful manner?

Positive and relaxed—maybe? I have a tough time with joyful, Coach."

"That is because you are forgetting who you are."

"Okay, who am I? You seem to know more about me than I do."

"You are part of the Creator. He created you in His likeness, and as I have mentioned before, you are here to learn. Your problems provide you with what you need to move forward—to advance in your understanding. When problems arise, you will be joyful because you will accept them as opportunities for advancement."

"Advancement to where? Am I getting a corner office with a view and a raise?"

"Better than that! You are getting an understanding of why you are here and what you may do with your life, if you wish to do so. City Bear, I know this is not easy. It is not supposed to be. This will help. I want you to think of a movie you have seen: *An Officer and a Gentleman*."

He paused, as if deep in thought, for a few seconds and continued, "Louis Gossett, Jr., the drill sergeant, played the role with every fiber of his being. He became the drill sergeant. When you looked at him, what came from his inner core was an outward expression of who he was, with no pretending. There was no doubt who he was, and he did not have to explain it. He did not start out being that character; he was someone very different, and though some may say he was pretending, if he did not become the drill sergeant in his inner core, he would not be able to express who he was without words. Right now, you can choose a similar transformation."

"To become Louis Gossett, Jr.? Coach, I can see the *Enquirer* headline: Chunky White Man Becomes Louis Gossett, Jr.!"

"You love to joke. You cannot help yourself. I do not know New Jersey, but I suspect there are many like you who live there."

"You're the one who told me not to take myself too seriously."

"City Bear, even I am not correct all the time. Let us get back to work. I want you to never again say in regard to losing weight, making money, having rewarding relationships, the job and life you want, that you will try. We have talked about this before. Now I want you to see it and make it happen with no more pretending. Today you begin being who you were meant to be, regardless of what is going on in your life circumstances. You will create the picture and accept only that picture of who you are every moment, whether awake or asleep. You are, right now, who you want to be, and as you think and act … you become. An oak, even when it is an acorn, knows it is an oak. You never realized your destination because you never saw yourself arriving; you were always on the way. You were always trying."

"Coach, how is trying easy different than trying?"

"Trying easy means you can already do whatever it is. Trying means you cannot do it yet!"

"Okay, so you're saying all I have to do is believe I am who I want to be and the changes will happen? Suppose I want to be a Major League Baseball player?"

"That is not realistic, and you know that. It is realistic to be fit, healthy, financially solvent, and able to enjoy the company of family and friends while helping to change the world. Besides, you are not interested in baseball."

"So it will only work if it is realistic?"

"That is correct, City Bear."

"How do I know what's realistic? I mean, maybe I could become the next Donald Trump."

"Do you want to be the next Trump?"

"Maybe Trump without the bad hairdo. I'm kidding. I would rather be who I am. That's what I want. To become who I am capable of being."

"There is no reason that cannot happen. It is up to you to rearrange your mind furniture. There are some pieces that need to be brought to the curb for garbage collection, while others need a little polishing, and for some pieces, you will replace what is worn or broken."

"That sounds possible, Coach."

"Thank you. I am glad I have your approval. City Bear, the first day we met, I asked you to write down your dreams, and today I'm asking you to be, every minute of your life, who you always wanted to be with no pretending."

"I remember thinking; how do I do that? I'm not at the weight I'd like to be and not in the physical condition I like, and I don't have the job or money I want or the family relationships I want. How can I see it differently when these things aren't reality? They're wishes!"

"Reality? City Bear, remember when we talked about illusion; what is real and what is not?"

"Yeah."

"Would you agree that much of reality is what we tell ourselves it is?"

"What do you mean?"

"If you have no money in your pocket and nothing in the bank, you are poor. Yes?"

"Okay, Coach, I'll go with that."

"If a man has a million dollars in a suitcase and it is his, he is rich. Yes?"

"Yeah."

"And if the man who has no money has the will and drive and a vision that he is already rich and works toward that goal, knowing it his destiny but he must work for it, is he poor?"

"Well, yeah, he still doesn't have the money."

"If the man with the million dollars believes that he does not deserve it and he will probably lose it, or even with the million, does not feel wealthy—that it is not enough—that he is lacking financially, is he rich?"

"Well, yeah, because he has the money in his hand now."

"That's the answer ... now!"

"What do you mean, Coach?"

"Now is always changing. What was now a second ago is no longer now. It is always changing, and the person whose thought process is positive, healthy, and successful changes their now every second, every millisecond, to a new now. The thought process defined by lack and concern is telling that person their now will only deteriorate. This style of thinking will not only make the person who uses it poor, it also causes ill health. It is in the changing of the now that defines who you are and who you will be."

"Coach, that is a very different way of looking at life."

"That is why you are here. If you thought like everyone else, you would have nothing to teach. There is a wonderful Native American story that illustrates my point. A baby eagle had fallen from its nest and was found by a farmer. The farmer put it in a pen with prairie chickens, and it was raised to think it was a prairie chicken. One day, after the eagle had become an adult, he saw a magnificent bird flying high in the sky and said to one of the prairie chickens, 'What is that beautiful bird?' The chicken responded, 'That is an eagle, the king of all birds. Because you are a prairie chicken, you will never be able to fly like an eagle. You will spend your life scratching for seeds and corn. That is what prairie chickens do.' And the eagle grew old and died never knowing that he was an eagle."

"I get it, Coach. A lot of us are eagles and we don't know it."

"Maybe there is hope for you, City Bear."

"Maybe there's hope? What kind of a thing is that to say? It sounds like I'm a little short on brain power."

He answered in a matter-of-fact tone, "When you realize you are an eagle, you will not be so easily insulted. Instead, you will laugh at the insult. You are doing fine. Remember, it is all about learning."

"I guess I have a lot to learn."

"We all do. That is where the fun is: the learning, the constant evolution, the ever changing now. The joy is in the process, once we learn to enjoy it; everything we do and think becomes part of the process."

"Coach, I feel like there's too much to learn and not enough time."

"If you lived a thousand lifetimes, there would not be enough time. What is important is now and what you do with your now. As long as you have a now, there is time to do something good for others. When you do something for someone, you change the world. You make it better than it was for that person. When enough people start doing good things for others, Mother Earth will begin to heal, because right deeds and right thinking brings about right results."

"What does healing Mother Earth have to do with good thoughts and actions toward others?"

"Nelson Mandela said, 'As we let our light shine, we unconsciously give other people permission to do the same. As we are liberated from our own fear, our presence automatically liberates others.' I know by being who you always wanted to be, and by including a focus on serving others, it becomes impossible to think or act in a manner that is not healthy and healing. When enough people begin thinking and acting in the service of others, the power of greed and selfishness will diminish, and actions will be taken to stop the pollution and heal our tiny planet."

"You're saying everything is connected."

"Of course it is! There is only so much air and water on earth, and if it were not constantly recycled, it would have been used up long ago. Other people used molecules of air and water in your body long before anyone began to think about history or civilization. Tomorrow night we will spend more time understanding our connection to each other."

"I still don't know if I totally get this."

"City Bear, this is your Tenth Gift: if you believe that you are part of the Creator and are always evolving toward your highest self and working toward that goal through your thoughts and actions, even if your life is presently not the way you want it to be, when you envision it and believe it to be the way you want it to be, your now draws it to you like a magnet."

"You're saying that you become what you think about?"

"Yes. But it is also a matter of focus and action. If you are not consistent in your thoughts and do not put your thoughts into action, the circuit to make the connection is never completed long enough to get the message through."

"Coach, I never realized how powerful our thoughts are!"

"I have one more story that may help you in your relationship with Star."

"Coach, I don't have a relationship with Star."

"City Bear, have you forgotten who I am?"

"Sorry, it's just that I don't have the quality relationship with Star I'd like to have. I hardly know her."

"What I believe you mean is you do not have the relationship you would like to have with Star now."

"Yeah."

"Remember that now is always changing," he said.

I was stunned. Coach was advising me how to improve my romantic relationship with what I believed to be the woman of my dreams. I felt like I had just scored a touchdown to win the Super Bowl, climbed Mount Everest, and won the lottery all at the same time.

I tried to concentrate as he continued. "When I traveled around the world learning about healing, I spent some time in London. I was on my way to a monastery, and a friend of the community had taken me to dinner at a very fine restaurant that had an area set aside for dancing. I enjoy observing and noticed that a young man, not particularly well dressed and not particularly good looking, was asking some of the prettiest women at the restaurant to dance. It was crowded, and the dance floor was very busy. I watched as he asked them to dance and was rejected over and over. I counted five rejections and thought: this man has courage. After each rejection, he would return to his drink at the bar, wait a few minutes, and continue the process. I was busy in conversation with the people at my table for about an hour and was ready to leave when I noticed that he was dancing with one of the best-looking women there. It appeared that she was enjoying herself."

"So, the young man envisioned himself dancing with a pretty woman first, in his mind. Next, he took focused action, even after getting rejected many times, and eventually, his thought became reality. Good story, Coach. *See my relationship with Star as if it's everything I want it to be.*

"City Bear, this afternoon, after your walk with Star, I want you to go back to your room and review your notes about who you always wanted to be. See if there are any changes based on our discussion, and if needed, make the appropriate changes. With practice, you will eliminate fear from your thoughts, and you will think of yourself as being who you always wanted to be and doing what you always wanted to do. Lao Tzu, considered by many to be one of the wisest men whoever lived, said, 'as you realize that all things change, there is nothing you will try to hold on to. If you aren't afraid of dying, there is nothing you cannot achieve.' So, as you write, see yourself smiling and enjoying the process with the knowledge that you have been chosen to help in healing the world and that all of us have limited time."

"Healing the world? You keep saying that, and it still worries me, and also, I am afraid of dying."

"You will not do it alone. You are going to have all the help you need, and it will come from the folks who see in you what they want to be. Just a few minutes ago, I quoted Mandela, and let me remind you of the second sentence in that quote: 'As we are liberated from our own fear, our presence automatically liberates others.' That will happen with you. You will have people help you because of who you are."

"Coach, you didn't answer the part about dying."

"Everyone is dying every day. The minute we are born, we are moving toward our death. People do not like to think of it that way, but it is true. Also, we have little control over whether we live one year or a hundred years, and though a hundred years may seem like a long time, it is not a pinhead on an ocean's horizon when compared with eternity. Again, City Bear, it is about adjusting your perspective."

I took a deep breath and said, "Okay, so I write down who I have always wanted to be, as if it has already occurred, and accept that by being who I always wanted to be, I will attract those people who will give me the help I need to change the world."

"Yes!"

"By the way, Coach, what is it exactly I am going to change about the world?"

"You will be told tomorrow night! And remember to make certain your heart is filled with a desire to help those who need your gifts."

"What gifts?"

"The gifts you will recognize when you stop being afraid."

"What am I afraid of?"

"Whatever it is that keeps you from being who you really are."

"Coach, you're giving me a headache."

"Maybe you need one. I hope your pain is minimal but sufficient for growth."

"Anything else, Coach?"

"Remember to forgive yourself for poor judgment; inconsideration of yourself and others; feelings of anger, resentment, and jealousy; desires for revenge; hurtful thoughts, words and actions, and anything you have done or failed to do that you are remorseful about."

"Why is it so important that I forgive myself?"

"We spoke about that yesterday. How quickly you forget. It is equally important that you forgive others who have harmed you. If you cannot forgive yourself, you cannot forgive others."

"Is that it?"

"Almost," he answered. "You have written what you want physically, mentally, spiritually, financially, as well as in your relationships with family, friends, and others. Now take those thoughts and make them a screenplay. Make a movie!"

"Make a movie?" I repeated.

"Yes! Edit the tape in your mind and splice it all together. See yourself physically, mentally, spiritually, financially, and in all relationships with others, as being the man you want to be. See fulfilling and rewarding relationships with your family, friends, co-workers, and enemies. Splice the film together and edit the movie to be what you want. You are the director, producer, and leading man. Once you have it all together, run the tape in your mind with as many details as you can. Do not forget to involve your senses: sight, hearing, touch, taste, and smell. Involve as many of your senses as possible. Throughout the movie, watch yourself as the main character being the person you always wanted to be without the fear of failure or success. As you watch the movie, feel a sense of joy and contentment, knowing you are fulfilling your purpose on Earth, and know your life has meaning. Also remember, you are going to make the world a better place for all its animals, plants and people. You will become part of the process to help to heal Mother Earth. To restore her lifeblood, the water we drink and the water that grows our food. To restore her lungs, which give us the air we breathe. Know you will be working with thousands, and eventually millions, of other stewards who want to draw out and destroy the poisons of pollution that have made our mother ill. I want you to smile in your heart, knowing that what you are doing is beyond good; it is holy and even more, it is sacred, and … it will be done.

"Many women will be involved in your work and the same principles that I have taught you, you will teach to them. The principles are exactly the same for men and women because we are all part of the Creator."

Again, I was aware of my heart pounding in my chest when I answered, "This sounds exciting and at the same time scary."

"Scary means fear. You do not need that anymore. Go with the excitement and encouragement of knowing you will be guided to do whatever it is that needs to be done, and the problems you will encounter are there because you need to learn from them. There is no need for fear. You are now working toward doing many of the good things that need to be done, and you will be guided along the way."

"Guided? Who's going to guide me?"

"You are! You already know the way but have not been able to see it because of your fear. As the fear evaporates, the way becomes clearer. You are going to be guided by that part of you that is connected to the Creator because you will ask for that guidance every day, and when you ask with a sincere mind and heart, your request is always honored. Again, those who see in you what they want to be will be drawn to you and want to help. As long as you are focused on doing what is in the best interest of serving others and not focused on serving yourself, you will complete your mission. In serving others, you will find your happiness, your contentment, and your reward. That is enough. Take a rest. I will see you at dinner."

Chapter Twenty

Star added, "I meant everything I said today!"

Kachinas and Whirlwinds

Star made a vegetarian casserole for lunch—noodles, cheese, peppers, onions, eggs, spinach, and broccoli. At least that's what I could identify. The main course was presented in a sea-green ceramic dish about six by twelve inches and four inches deep. She had heated the same bread we had for breakfast, and I enjoyed it just as much the second time.

We ate alone. She did most of the talking and spoke about a trip to Santa Fe she made to meet a girlfriend from college. She told me about the open-air, old-fashioned farmers' market, the art galleries, and the great food she enjoyed at back street restaurants where the locals ate. She was animated and enthusiastic, and her energy was contagious. Everything she did sounded like fun, and her descriptions made me wish I had been there with her. I nodded and smiled appropriately and didn't have to act interested, because I was.

Star told me that the Native American people in the area call Santa Fe "Santa Fake" because they think it's too glitzy and phony. She said, "Many Indians think white people have too much money and it ruins them. It makes them forget we are all connected. Some of them measure people only by their bank account. These same people feel entitled because they're wealthy. Often they treat others, especially Native Americans, with a lack of respect."

She seemed pretty down on pahanas, the Hopi word for Caucasians, when she added, "Not all white people are that way. You're not like that. There are good and bad in all races."

I was grateful for the compliment and knew I would do anything I could to maintain her approval.

"We can talk more about Santa Fe, if you would like to, during our walk. It will take me about fifteen minutes to get the kitchen tidy, so would 1:15 work for you?"

"Sure, 1:15 is great."

"Stop by the kitchen, and we will leave from there."

I returned to my room, washed my hands and face, brushed my teeth, and checked my smile in the mirror. The last thing I wanted to do was smile at Star and have a gooey piece of spinach between my teeth.

I have no idea how she did it so quickly, but when I stopped by the kitchen, everything was clean and neat and she had changed her jeans, blouse, and boots. She wore a loose-fitting blue cotton dress with a wide, matching leather belt decorated with blue, yellow, and green beads that formed primitive pictures of animals—pictures that could have been made on a cave wall thousands of years ago. The belt was snug fitting and accentuated her figure. Her blue moccasins were decorated with the same pictures as the belt.

When I arrived, she was drying the last dish; she placed it in the cupboard and said, "Are you ready?"

That was a pleasantry. She knows I'm ready. I nodded.

She walked toward the back of the house and I followed. We walked side by side past the field of wildflowers. When Coach and I went for our walks, we always turned west. I was ready to make the turn and saw that she turned east. I had never walked in that direction; the landscape seemed more barren. There were fewer shrubs and cactus, and we walked toward what appeared to be a dried-up riverbed.

"Apache men often walk the arroyos looking for cottonwood. They take it to trading posts for sale to Kachina carvers. Do you know about Kachinas?"

"No," I answered.

"Kachinas are dolls that are very important to many Native American people. Some folks call them Katsinas and some prefer Kachinas."

I was fascinated by her story about the Apaches and the dolls, and as we continued our walk, following the riverbed, I asked, "What are the dolls used for?"

"Historically, Kachinas were masked and costumed Native American dancers who represented various spirits and elements of life. A Kachina could represent a warrior, a singer, a clown—lots of characters. Oftentimes Kachinas look like animals: eagles, bear, and deer—all kinds of animals. There are also Kachinas for the sun, moon, stars, and Earth."

"But what do you do with them?"

"The Kachina was used as a teaching tool. It is said that the spirits taught the elders, who taught others through the representations in the Kachina dolls. Today they are still used in religious ceremonies, and many people collect them as an art form. I have over thirty dolls. Some are from my great-grandmother and were given to her by her grandmother. They are treasures."

"Why cottonwood? Why do they make the dolls from cottonwood?"

"It's easy to carve and sand."

We walked for about twenty minutes, and neither of us said anything. I was enjoying just being with her and didn't feel the need or urge to talk. The occasional breeze felt refreshing, and I could taste the salt from my sweat on my lips.

We walked toward a depression in the riverbed that, upon closer inspection, was a hole probably dug by the rushing water of a desert storm. I noticed something white poking out the side of the hole and initially thought it was some kind of shell. I pried it loose and saw that it was a shard of pottery.

"Neat! Do you know what that is?"

"No," I answered.

"That's Anasazi pottery. I can tell from the design."

"Okay, so who were the Anasazi?"

"They are the ancient ones. They lived in the Four Corners area of the Southwestern United States from about 1200 BC to 1300 AD. They were cliff dwellers. Rather than call them the Anasazi, many Native Americans prefer to call them the Ancient Ones."

I handed her the shard and asked, "Is it okay to take this?"

"Not unless you make an offering."

"What kind of offering?"

"Cornmeal, money, tobacco."

After answering, she waited about two seconds and continued, "Cornmeal is probably the easiest. Get some cornmeal and go out into the desert and find a plant. It can be a bush or a cactus, any living plant. Put the pottery in front of the plant and say, 'I would like to take this piece of pottery, but first I want to make an offering.' Place the cornmeal next to the plant, and then you can take the pottery and there won't be any problems."

"What do you mean problems?"

"Whirlwinds. The Ancient Ones must be treated with respect, and by making the offering and asking, you are being respectful."

"Do I have to make the offering now?"

"No. The Ancient Ones know what is in your heart. Before you return home, find a place in the desert that feels right and make your offering. It will be okay."

I put the piece of broken pottery in my pocket and contemplated: *whirlwinds! I wonder what that means, but I'm not going to ask, because it doesn't sound good. This is a little unusual. I'm from Hudson County, New Jersey, one of the most densely populated areas in the United States. I don't know about the Ancient Ones or making an offering to keep away the whirlwinds. Maybe I'll just put the piece of pottery back.*

Her voice interrupted my musing when she said, "It's okay. Stop worrying. You will make your offering, and the shard will be your treasure."

I didn't answer. I felt like I wasn't reacting like a "real man" by being tentative, and decided to restore some of my masculinity by nodding.

We had walked for about two hours, but it seemed like ten minutes. *I would be happy to walk for another two hours, but I knew that enough had been shared and it was time to get back to the ranch.*

When we turned to head back, she took my hand and held it—although she didn't look at me. She continued to hold my hand as we walked toward the ranch, and after about ten minutes, she said, "I am not sure where this is going, Andy, but from the time I heard your voice on the phone, I knew I wanted to meet you. I do all the research for Uncle, and long before we spoke, I knew a great deal about you. I know that I am considerably younger than you, but that does not matter to me. I want to help you complete your mission, and I know the reasons you were chosen. Uncle has great faith in you."

When she called me Andy and not City Bear, it sounded like we had been friends before Coach had given me my Indian name. It sounded endearing, and I liked it.

I was thinking again about the pottery ceremony, when she said, "Stop worrying. It's okay! Remember that the Ancient Ones know what is in your heart, and they know that you will respect their ways."

The sun had lost some of its searing heat by the time we reached the ranch. She stopped at the kitchen door, turned, gave me a peck on the cheek, looked in my eyes, smiled, and said, "I will see you at dinner." Followed by, "I enjoyed the walk."

I never expected the handholding, her private thoughts about wanting to meet me, and the peck. When I returned to my room, I sat at the desk chair for at least a half hour in amazement. I reviewed every word of our conversation during the walk and remembered the jolt I felt when she took my hand. Over and over, I repeated her words, "I'm not sure where this is going, Andy, but from the time I heard your voice on the phone, I knew I wanted to meet you."

I decided to write some notes for entry later into my journal, and took a shower and napped before dinner. This was my fifth day at the ranch, and yet it seemed like a lifetime. Already I knew I was different than when I first arrived. I wondered what the initiation ceremony would be like, and my mission—though I had no idea what it was— made me nervous. The late-afternoon air had cooled the room, and the smell of the dry earth had entered through the screened window. I remember feeling more alive than I had felt in a very long time, and when I checked my watch, I had fifteen minutes until dinner.

Coach was seated when I arrived, and he asked me about my walk with Star. I knew the question was a formality and that he already knew the answer, but I played along. I told him about finding the pottery and her informing me about the need to have a ceremony. Star arrived with the soup and a pile of warm flatbread. I was getting used to soup for dinner, and tonight's choice was potato barley, and it was, as usual, outstanding.

He didn't have much to say, while Star entertained us with stories about her first days at the ranch and her initial thoughts that the ranch was beyond repair. She was very funny, and this was a side of her I hadn't seen. I found her conversation charming and endearing. Not that I wasn't charmed before, but her stories added a dimension that turned up the flame of my infatuation.

I asked Star if I could help clean up, and as usual, she told me that she was happy to do so and guests may not help with kitchen chores.

She knew that I just wanted to be with her, even if it was to clean the dishes, and for some reason she had decided that we needed some space. I knew she was right, and when Coach said he would be going to visit some friends, I knew I'd be visiting his library and living room.

About an hour and a half later, Star came into the living room and brought me a cup of coffee, as well as some peanuts in a dish. She turned to leave, and in what seemed like an afterthought, turned back and said, "I meant everything I said today."

I watched her walk toward the door and couldn't think of anything to say. I had read enough for the day and decided to return to my room. I opened the journal and wrote:

Day 5

Today I learned to think of all my tension and worries floating from my fingertips to be burned on the glow of the burning sage incense.

Coach then taught me some new weight-training exercises and advised me to keep a record of my repetitions and amount of weight used, so that each week I can assess my progress and plan accordingly.

Next, he presented me with admonitions to stop being a scared rabbit; to remember that I am an eagle; not to be afraid of challenges; and to know that I am part of the Creator, as well as that everything and everyone is connected. And then given the Tenth Gift—I am a part of the Creator.

If I believe I am always evolving toward my highest self and working toward that goal, through my thoughts and actions, even if my life is presently not the way I want it to be. Then, when I envision it—believe it to be the way I want it to be—and give thanks, my now draws it to me like a magnet.

Coach also said, "One hundred years is not a pinhead on an ocean's horizon compared to eternity."

Next, he asked me to make a movie of who I always wanted to be physically, mentally, spiritually, financially, as well as in all my relationships, and to play the movie in my mind every night before I go to sleep and every morning when I awake.

Today's walk with Star included my finding an Anasazi pottery shard and her explaining to me why I needed to complete a ceremony and make an offering before I can take it. She also taught me about Kachinas, held my hand on the way back to the ranch, and throttled my limbic system into overdrive when she told me that it didn't matter that I was older than she.

I closed the journal, turned off the light, and fell asleep thinking of Star's face, as she talked to me in the dry riverbed about Kachinas and the Ancient Ones.

I had been asleep for a couple of hours when I awoke in a sweat. I'd been dreaming, and in the dream, a huge white tractor-trailer truck was careening down a mountain while the driver was slumped over the steering wheel. He looked like an Indian, because he had braids, but I couldn't see his face. I didn't know if he had fallen asleep or something had happened that incapacitated him. There was a sign on the side of the truck that read in big black letters: Responsible Trucking.

I was riding in the truck and yelling, as loudly as I could, for the man to wake up. When that didn't work, I pushed him, hoping that would help. He didn't budge, and we were going faster and faster, heading for a city full of people. Finally, I grabbed him by the hair on the top of his head and pulled him back. When I looked at his face, I saw it was my face—that's when I woke up with my undershirt-wringing wet.

I was shaking and could feel my heart pounding in my ears. I tried to figure out what my subconscious was telling me, but I didn't get it. What I did know was that something was wrong, very wrong, and the little man who lives deep within my psyche had spoken to me in pictures—it was then up to me to figure out what it all meant. I wondered if my apprehension was related to my concerns about fulfilling my mission.

I couldn't get back to sleep, and finally, after what seemed like hours, drifted off only to hear the greeting of the bells. *I'm exhausted! I don't know how I'll make it through my final day.*

Chapter Twenty-one

*Kindness to others as well as to me
is something rarely taught.*

Tony Soprano and John Rambo

When I entered the stone room he was already seated, his eyes were open, and he smiled at me.

Coach never smiled at me before we meditated. I felt uneasy, like a kid whose father always yells at him and one day he comes home from school and his father doesn't yell, he smiles.

He followed the smile with an announcement. "I mentioned yesterday that today would be the most important day of your life, and I meant it. **Your Eleventh Gift is: The only thing that matters is kindness.** You will bring happiness and joy into the lives of the people with whom you interact by your kindness, and many of these people will also be the same people who will help you with your mission."

I was deep in thought about his words, "help you with your mission," and had to force myself to listen as he continued, "You are Catholic, and I had not mentioned it, but saying the Rosary provides many of the same meditation benefits as using a mantra. In order for it to work with the Rosary, you have to say the various prayers without focusing on the words. When you do not make a conscious effort to think of the words, their sounds become a mantra, and you get the same benefits."

Interesting—another example of how everything is connected. After meditation, we exercised and followed the same pattern we started earlier in the week, except he added two kettlebell exercises and another yoga form. I continued to be impressed with his strength, agility, and the ease with which he completed the exercises.

It was fun watching him, and I'm embarrassed to admit it, though he was much younger, he had become a role model, and I wanted to imitate his composure and physical prowess.

When I completed my last set, he said, "In the short time you have been here, you have made great progress with your meditation and exercise program. See you at breakfast."

Gee, coming from Coach, that was a very big deal. His approval had become very important to me, and I repeated his compliment silently to myself at least three or four times. It felt good.

A number of times during the morning, I reflected back to his Eleventh Gift and his advice about what really matters, and thought about it a good part of the morning.

At breakfast today, Star seemed distant. She smiled, initiated conversation, and completed the breakfast ritual in the same manner as the other days. I could feel something was different. Before, she was naturally cheerful, and now I felt she was trying to appear that way.

He stayed at the table longer than usual, and when Star got up to remove the dishes, he said, "I will see you at the sandy patch in fifteen minutes."

I had showered before breakfast. So, I washed my hands and face, brushed my teeth, and made the bed.

As usual, he was waiting for me, and when I sat next him, he said, "City Bear, today I will take everything you have been taught and add to it to create something that will be refreshing, restorative, healthy, and fun. You are going to learn to sing and dance in your heart."

"Maybe I'll get good enough to try out for *Dancing with the Stars.*"

"I am going to ignore that. You will learn to sing and dance in your heart without anyone knowing it but you. You are going to be set free from the worries and troubles that have caused you pain, and after you learn the process for attaining your own freedom, you are going to help others to free themselves from their worries, concerns, and unhappiness."

"That's quite a statement. Today I'm going to be set free. It makes me feel like I've been some kind of caged animal."

"You have been! You did not start out that way, but like most of us, we end up in one kind of cage or another. The strongest cages have no bars. They are made of rules that you will follow so that you can get your reward."

"Get my reward? You make it sound like I'm a pigeon performing tricks for a kernel of corn."

"Yes, that is very close to what I mean."

I figured he was alluding to work and said, "Some people love what they do for a living. I don't think they're pigeons."

"They are not. I am not referring to them. My perception is directed to those who dislike what they do and lie to themselves. We began discussing this subject earlier in the week when we spoke about getting crumbs from the table."

Coach stopped speaking, took a breath, and said, "When we serve at the whim of others who have little or no regard for our well-being, health, or happiness, and perform a task or tasks that we do not enjoy doing, a part of us becomes numb."

"Okay, that description fits most people. So?"

"In some cases, we complete the required tasks to keep a roof over our family and food on the table, and many of us pretend that we like what we dislike. When we deny our feelings and convince ourselves that we like what we dislike, we become the equivalent of human pigeons who perform a trick for a reward."

"It's easy for you to say, Coach, because you don't have a wife or kids who count on you for a paycheck. You can call good people pigeons, but I think they are heroes because they put their families first and themselves second. They're not pigeons, they're heroes, and maybe know a lot more than you about sacrifice."

"City Bear, your tone tells me you are angry. You have learned that all anger is the product of fear. What are you afraid of?"

"I don't think I'm afraid of anything. But maybe I'm afraid that you don't understand what I've tried to do for my family and me. I always put them first; I know about sacrifice. I've done a lot of things I didn't want to do and kissed up to a lot of people I don't like because I had to for my family."

"And where has it brought you, City Bear?"

"Here?"

"No. What does your life look like? Where are you? Are you healthy? I know you are overweight and have a blood pressure challenge. You have told me that money has always been a problem. Your children are angry with you and your marriage is over. How did the anxiety and worry about your job affect not only your health but also the health of your family relationships?"

"So, what you have explained to me to be self-sacrifice, for the well-being of others, appears not to be in your best interest or that of your family, and your self-delusion has cost you and them a hefty price."

"I don't know how I could have done it differently," I said, trying to defend myself.

"You could have taken the time to find something that you enjoyed doing, and if there was not enough money at first, then everyone would have had to cut back and live on less."

"I guess I was afraid to do that because I wanted them to love me. I believed that by giving them what I thought they wanted, I'd be loved."

"Did it work?"

"No. My life is a disaster. A train wreck."

"City Bear, by being kind to yourself, you make it easier to be kind to others because you are happy. Being kind includes self-discipline, self-reflection, right occupation, enough sleep, and forgiving yourself … there is more. But that is a start."

I was mentally replaying his advice to be kind to myself and thought, *Kindness to others and ourselves is something rarely taught or spoken about, and yet it's what most people will remember about us when we're gone. They will ask themselves, "Was he or she kind to me?"*

I had been lost in my thoughts about kindness when I heard him continue. "Okay. Enough. City Bear, I believe you understand the pigeon metaphor. Now I am going to teach you to sing and dance in your heart, but first we have to do some preparatory work."

"What kind of preparatory work?"

"Be patient. First, I want you to know that you are on Earth to be happy and to complete your mission. We create most of our unhappiness by incorrect thoughts and actions. Thoughts and actions that are not in keeping with who we really are place us on a lower frequency. Many thoughts are motivated by anxiety, fear, and worry that there will not be enough; that there will be a lack of something. The lack can be food, money, recognition, power, or love. It always has to do with a fear of not enough. The emotions focused on lack work toward bringing about just what we are worried about—lack. We think lack and we get lack. We have spoken about this before."

"Okay, so what do I do to think and act in a new way that will allow me to not be concerned with lack?"

"You will not think of lack if you are grateful. It is so easy to forget how much we have. **Your Twelfth and last gift is the Gift of Gratitude: You are encouraged to give thanks all day long. Every minute of the day, every second of the day … give thanks!**"

"Thanks for what?"

"Everything!"

"Even the people who make me angry and want to hurt me?"

"You need to give thanks for them most of all, because they

provide you with opportunities to grow, change, and improve. They give you the opportunity to raise the frequency of your being so that you can see, hear, feel, and know things that presently are unavailable to you. As you give thanks for what you have, you also give thanks for what you do not have, because you can look forward only to that which is not realized."

"So I will learn to sing and dance in my heart by giving thanks?"

"Giving thanks brings you to the door. And you open it by saying to the Creator, 'Thank you for letting me be part of this life, with its beauty and ugliness, with its love and hate, with its wealth and poverty, with its health and sickness. Thank you for allowing me to take my place in this world, which may be one of many worlds, and thank you for allowing me to see, hear, touch, taste, smell, work, love, and die. Thank you for allowing me to experience sunrises and sunsets, works of art, flowers, the birds and animals, the variety of people and cultures, the lakes and streams, the mountains, the oceans. Thank you for the ability to think, because thinking is the seed of all action, and by changing my thinking, I can change my actions, and by changing my actions, I can change those parts of my life that I want to improve.'"

I liked what he had to say and responded, "If I am a pigeon, performing for a kernel of corn, I will change my thoughts and actions until I am an eagle soaring majestically in a boundless blue sky."

"Now you are singing and dancing in your heart, City Bear."

"It sounds so simple, Coach!"

"It is and it is not. It takes practice. Lots and lots of practice, and just when you think you have it, sometimes you will feel like you have to start over again. You will say or do something that will make you feel you have made no progress. Enlightenment does not happen in a day. It is a gradual process, and sometimes we get it and sometimes we do not."

"I feel like it's going to take me a long time to 'get it.'"

"I am very pleased you put it that way. Because enlightenment, for most of us, takes many lifetimes to achieve, but there is another way."

"Are you going to tell me, or do we have to do some preparatory work for that too?"

"I sense impatience. Take a deep breath and stop trying so hard. Everything will be accomplished in the right time and at the right pace."

I took a deep breath and said, "Okay, I'm listening and trying ... but not too hard to be patient."

"City Bear, when you give thanks all day long, remember to think of yourself singing and dancing in your heart, and as you do, see yourself smiling. Know that the effects of your smile are going throughout your body like a light spreading from your heart to every corner of your body. Think of the light bathing all of your body's cells in joy and laughter, and feel the peace."

"That's it?"

"There is more, and we will get there."

"This is my last day—will we get there today?" I asked.

"If you don't stop," he said, "I am going to send you back to New Jersey and you will have to wait for an open week and start over."

"Sorry, Coach." I had been chastised and was okay with it.

"When you smile, as you watch yourself sing and dance in your heart, and as you joyfully give thanks, your body chemistry will change. The change will be visible to others as well as yourself, and you will radiate joy and peace. Look in the mirror. If your eyes are not joyful and laughing, you are not smiling in your heart. Practice until you see it."

I was thinking about how singing and dancing creates joy, and for the first time in my life, I thought, *the Creator wants us to have a good time on Earth. Sure, there will always be problems, but He gave us singing and dancing to allow us to feel joy in spite of our challenges.*

"Watch the Dalai Lama. Aside from when he is thinking deeply about something, his eyes are almost always smiling. They are joyful. That does not mean he cannot feel lack or hurt, anger or sadness, and his eyes will radiate those feelings. He does not get stuck there and instead chooses to see these emotions in a new way—to see them as tools for practice and growth."

"I can't compare myself to the Dalai Lama. I spent most of my life as an administrator for a public school system."

"I am not asking you to compare yourself, but rather to think of him as a model. If it is easier, because you are Catholic, you may wish to think of a picture of the Sacred Heart of Jesus. The picture where His heart is visible and radiates light and His smile is joyful and benevolent."

It is very interesting that a Buddhist would know about the Sacred Heart of Jesus icon, and at the same time, I was really tired. I blurted out, like a ten-year-old with attention deficit disorder, "I can't do this. I'm not that good! This is too much. I think Theophane made a mistake at the train station and was supposed to meet someone from Rhode Island or Connecticut, where people are more civil and polite. When I'm angry enough, I want to be Tony Soprano and do unto others what they deserve. When I'm really ticked off, I've asked myself what would John Rambo do in my situation, and I can get really ugly."

"Tony has panic attacks and high blood pressure. You have had both. It does not seem that the approach he uses to cope with anger has worked for him, and it has not worked for you."

"How do you know about Tony Soprano?"

"That is enough discussion about a TV program that is make-believe. You need to practice remembering who you are—with no pretending—and remember to be thankful for those who persecute you, because they allow you to practice compassion and understanding. That does not mean you should not protect yourself if someone tries to hurt you physically, financially, emotionally, or spiritually. We have spoken about this before. You are always encouraged to protect yourself—in doing so, you must be careful of your intent. If your intent is to protect yourself, and if someone is hurt in your doing so, they have brought about this reaction by problems related to their thoughts and actions. You do not have to be a doormat, and neither should you be looking for a fight all the time. By the way, I am also a fan of John Rambo, although he needs to meditate more. He needs more quiet time!"

"Coach, what you're talking about isn't something I'm sure I can do or want to do."

"That is up to you. Everything is. You may want to ask yourself the benefit you have realized by doing things your way. If you are satisfied, do as you have done. But I do not think you are happy with the way you have lived your life."

"You're right. Maybe I'm afraid I can't change, and all this teaching and time will be wasted because I don't have what it takes to do what you expect of me."

"City Bear, Theophane did not make a mistake. I have told you this before, but you have not accepted my support. I believe you can do this.

"Today we are going to have two sessions. The session tonight will be the culmination of all our work. It will also serve as your initiation ceremony. Think about what we have discussed in these last six days, and tonight, if you have any questions, I will answer them. Tonight you will get your final instructions and mission."

"Mission. You keep saying that, and it sounds like I'm in the army."

"You are—a very different kind of army. You will understand more tonight. For now, go and do what you want: nap, walk, snack, or read. There are sandwiches in the refrigerator and coffee and soup on the stove. Help yourself. There will be no formal dinner tonight. Come to the fire pit at 8:00, and bring a jacket. Do not wear shoes or socks. Star will be with us for the ceremony."

The mention of her name brought back thoughts of our walk in the desert and also the dream that followed. I felt uneasy. I decided to go to my room and make some journal entries. I opened the book and wrote:

Day 6

What I learned this morning:

- The Rosary is a mantra, and I can use it as a form of meditation.
- I will be taught to sing and dance in my heart.
- I have come to realize that I have spent a good part of my life not being kind to myself. That by giving my family the material things they wanted, I'd be loved. What they really wanted was my time and for me to be happy.
- Asking myself what Tony Soprano or John Rambo would do when angry is not productive.

Gift Eleven

The only thing that matters is kindness to others, with whom I interact, and myself.

Gift Twelve

I remember him saying, "Your Twelfth Gift is the Gift of Gratitude, and you are encouraged to give thanks all day long. Every minute of the day, every second of the day, give thanks!"

I closed the journal and thought that the uncertainty of the initiation ceremony had me on edge. All I could do was wait and hope that I didn't do or say anything to embarrass myself. I decided, before showering, to go for my last walk in the desert before returning home, and I noticed how I had changed. I had become part of my surroundings and was no longer a stranger. My senses of sight, hearing, and smell had become keener, and I felt comfortable with silence. In fact, I now thought of silence as a friend who could be counted on in times of need.

When I returned, I was hungry. I took half a ham-and-cheese

sandwich, corn soup, and lemonade from the refrigerator. I turned the burners on low for the soup and coffee and sat by myself at the kitchen table. I felt a sense of separation and wondered why we weren't eating together on my last night.

I was tired from the week's activities, and after the shower, I took a nap. This time there were no dreams about trucks or Indians, just beautiful, restorative sleep, and I when I awoke, it was 6:30 PM. I washed my face and hands at the kitchen sink, heated and poured a cup of coffee, added some milk, and took it with me. I had just enough time to straighten up the room. I dressed in fresh clothes and felt anxious and energized at the same time. The room was neat and clean, and when I closed the door to leave, I knew that in the next few hours, if what Coach said became reality, I would be changed forever and never be able to return to my former self.

Chapter Twenty-two

We are special because the Creator's breath is within us!

The Initiation

When I arrived at the fire pit, I was glad I wore a jacket. After the sun went down, it got cold. When I arrived, Coach and Star were already there, and the fire was blazing. The pair sat on a small, brightly colored blanket similar to those in the Stone Room. Next to Star sat an elderly man with a dark and wrinkled face and braids that touched the top of his chest. A large animal-hide drum stood sentry-like in front of him, and in his right hand, he held one drumstick with a large felt tip the size of a marshmallow. Star introduced him as her uncle, Thomas, and said that he would be with us throughout the ceremony.

There was one other blanket that completed the circle around the fire, and Coach motioned for me to sit. He had not said a word, and he looked intently at the fire as if it were going to tell him a secret. I sat and crossed my legs.

Star looked absolutely beautiful. She wore jeans, a pink cotton blouse, and a buckskin jacket, and her jet-black hair hung loose to her waist. She and Coach were barefoot.

Coach began, "Tonight you will get your directions for your mission, and tonight you will understand the importance of changing yourself, so you can help heal yourself, help others, and assist in the healing of Mother Earth. Tonight will be the most important time of your life, second only to your birth and death. Tonight you will understand."

"Understand what?"

He ignored me and said, "Watch the fire." Then he asked, "What do you see?"

Here we go again! I had had enough of the what do you see, what do you hear questions. I didn't answer.

"Before the fire, there was a tree; before the tree, a seed—on and on all the way back to the first seed and the first tree. Before the first seed, there was only love—pure, radiant love. It filled the expanse of the universe. Love wanted to express itself, so it became seeds, trees, flowers, insects, fish, animals, and finally, us. The fire we are watching is warming our bodies and the result of the first seed. It grew not from a tree, but from love. Love tells everything how to grow and be."

Coach was matter-of-fact. His presentation held no room for question or doubt. He seemed to be explaining what he knew to be the truth, and he wanted to share his knowledge.

"The difference between us and the insects, trees, plants, earth, and water is that we can think in ways that are an expression of the love. The animals also can love, but not like us. We are special because the Creator's breath is within us. We are special because we are the most like the source of all love … the Creator."

I listened, and his words made me feel holy, as if I were a part of something very important, and I felt honored to be in the presence of this very unusual man and his enchanting housekeeper.

"We have the ability to do something the plants, trees, insects, and animals cannot. We can be kind to others who are not kind to us. We can return hatred and lies with compassion. We are the highest of God's creations. Many have forgotten who they are and have acted toward others and themselves in ways that are destructive. Some of those actions have poisoned our air, water, and earth. Members of the group we call mankind have often not lived up to their name and instead been unkind and have killed untold millions in the name of their god, who, they believe, is better than the god of the people they have killed."

As he spoke, he never looked at me. He looked directly into the fire, as if the fire was telling him what to say. We had been together for about fifteen minutes, and already I thought: *the picture of this night will never fade from my mind.*

"Man at his worst destroys, and at his best is compassionate and forgiving. When man forgives, he receives more of the Creator's breath, and it heals him and allows him to bring healing to others by his example. The greatest healers do nothing except be who they are. That is enough, because the Creator's breath works through them. It is the breath, not the healer that heals. The healer is a conduit for the breath. The breath is also known as the Spirit ... because it cannot be seen."

"Coach, this is very heavy stuff. My father was a plumber and my mother a homemaker. I didn't go to Harvard or Yale. I'm a regular guy. All this stuff about God's breath is a stretch for me. This is heavy."

"Actually, it is quite light. The more you understand what I mean about the Creator's breath, the more you will realize the power of compassion and forgiveness—two actions rooted in love. There are those who feel His breath in them every second of every day, and they are enlightened—or better said, they become light or in the light."

"I'm going to give it my best, Coach, but I still don't think I'm the right guy."

"You have told me that a number of times, and I heard you the first time. Do not tell me again unless you wish to leave now."

I was angry with myself for continuing to whine.

"You are not expected to know everything. You are in the process of learning, and the learning will take time and work. For the last six days, you have been taught to question, observe, listen, and think in ways that were not familiar to you. Your education will continue tonight, and you will have six months to practice what you have learned, as well as work on the completion of your mission. You will return here in six months, and more of the details will be provided for you at that time."

"I'm not sure I can do that, Coach. I'm not sure I can get here in six months."

"You will take one day at a time, and you will not only be back but return every year for the next three years."

"Why three years?"

"By then, you and the others who have been chosen to heal the Earth will have accomplished their missions, or Mother Earth will not have healed and it will be too late."

"Too late for what?"

"Too late to save the world as we know it."

"Enough talking. It is time to sing and dance. Singing and dancing are switches that will allow more of God's breath to enter you. After tonight, you will more fully understand what I mean when I tell you to sing and dance in your heart."

They stood up, and I followed. He began to chant. As directed, I didn't wear shoes.

"When you dance, he said, "you pat Mother Earth, as you might lovingly pat your mother, and you tell her that, though you may not have visited her recently, you have not forgotten her."

The drum began its cadence, and Uncle Thomas nodded with the beat. He had not said a word, and I wondered if he spoke English.

Coach then continued, "When you dance without shoes on the ground, there is nothing between you and Mother Earth, and she feels your pulse and your rhythm, and it joins with her heartbeat. As we sing and dance, we become one with her, and nothing else matters or exists. When we return to her, we return to ourselves, and there is no pretending. We are home. We know who we are, and we are the visible expression of perfect love. You are the Creator's breath given life through Mother Earth, and all males, including you and me, are His sons, and Star and all females, His daughters."

Coach and Star were standing, and he motioned for me to stand. He started to dance to the beat of the drum, and as he danced, Star and I joined him around the fire. Then he began singing in a low-pitched monotone that sounded more like a prayer than a song:

"My mother and I are one,

My mother and I are one,

My mother and I, my mother and I,

My mother and I are one."

Star and I joined Coach in his clockwise dance around the fire as Thomas drummed.

Coach continued:

"My father and I are one,

My father and I are one,

My father and I, my father and I,

My father and I are one."

My eyes weren't focused on anything, and the dance was in rhythm with the words and the beat of the drum. He sang:

"You and I are one,

You and I are one,

You and I, you and I,

You and I are one."

I felt the earth under my bare feet and seemed connected, as we danced, to a force far greater than anything I had ever experienced.

"All of us are one,

All of us are one,

All of us, all of us,

All of us are one."

As we danced, we repeated the words. By the second time, I knew what was coming next, and I sang without hesitation. As the night unfolded, he varied the dance from clockwise to counterclockwise and back again, as the singing and drumming moved us like an invisible engine. Time was unimportant. I was in communion with Mother Earth, Coach, Star, the wind, the night, the moon, the stars, and the sound of the drum. It was overwhelmingly beautiful, and the sounds and movement brought me as close to ecstasy as I've ever experienced.

I had no idea how long we danced, but it must have been hours, because the huge fire had died and become smoldering embers when I heard him say, "It is time for your mission."

He asked Star and me to take our seats. Thomas placed the drumstick on the ground and sat silently.

"City Bear, Mother Earth needs to breathe easier. The poisons in the air and water are killing her, and her breathing has become difficult. She has to rid herself of these toxins, and she is doing so by changing the weather patterns. The polar ice caps are melting so that there can be more pure water to dilute the poisons. We can help her breathing by planting more trees, as well as by stopping the pollution. Too many trees have been cut down, and she relies on the plants, trees, and tiny sea creatures in the oceans to clean her lungs. They are polluted and congested.

Your mission is to create a shift in how people think. Your are going to change yourself and in the process, help others to change how they feel about themselves, their relationships and their role on Earth. You are going to teach them, through your books and seminars, that we are all connected and that the fate of our planet depends on their willingness to take responsibility for its survival. That the fate of our planet depends on their willingness to become actively involved in changing how we do business, treat each other, and care for our finite resources: especially air and water.

"Coach, that job seems way beyond me. I wouldn't know where to begin."

"You will not do it alone. You will be guided, but you will be the conduit to make it happen. His love will do it through you."

I was shaking my head in disbelief when he continued, "I want you to hold the intention in your mind to help Mother Earth to heal and also, help others to forgive themselves, and bring about the process of creating heaven on Earth. In your daily actions, you will be led to people who can help heal the world and because of their interaction with you, they will want to do it. You could never do this alone—by living what you have learned many others will join in your efforts. Programs will be established that do not exist and the power behind this movement will be the Creator's love. You will ask your readers to make a commitment to change something about themselves that has been a lifelong concern. You will also ask them to do something, large or small, to improve our world, even if it is for only one person. You will ask them to complete these tasks within forty days of reading your book. And finally, you will invite them to let you know what they have done for themselves and others by emailing you at your website.

Do not doubt the power of the Creator. Miracles happen every day and I want you to be part of a miracle.

I was about to whine and decided not to go there. "Man up!" I said to myself, and as I thought of seeing Star again, Coach said, "Your instructions will follow concerning your return in six months."

"Can I contact you?"

"Only if you really need to. I want you to trust that everything will work out successfully and in a manner beyond your wildest dreams."

"How many folks will be invited to come here?"

"You are the first. As I mentioned, there will be two more. The next initiate is a woman, and the last a child who has been given a very special talent. All initiates have met with Theophane and received a book similar to yours. By the way, the book has been placed in your room, and I would like you to sign it on the next open space on the last page. Leave it on the desk. Only your book contains all of the names of those who have passed our tests and taken up the challenge of changing themselves for the purpose of changing the world. The pages of names will be removed from your book and placed in the book of the woman when she is ready to sign. The same process for the child."

I wondered why there would be only two more initiates, and once again, he answered my thought.

"The next initiate will teach the world they are 90 percent spirit and 10 percent body. Through her, they will learn they are spiritual beings that have been given an earthly body so that they can learn and help others to learn. She is a very unusual woman, and though she is very attractive, her real beauty is in her spirit. When she was a young woman, she was in a car accident and had clinically died for about eight minutes. She experienced the loving energy of a force beyond human comprehension, which she calls the God Energy. Since there is no time and space beyond the physical body, she was also encoded with volumes of information and wisdom from the perspective of the highest consciousness."

I wanted him to stop. My emotional and intellectual circuits were frying like eggs in a skillet. I was thinking: *encoded with volumes of information and wisdom? What does that mean and how's it done?*

He knew it was too much for me and I was in over my head when he said, "City Bear, please take a deep breath and listen. Your anxiety is interfering with your thought processing. Just listen!"

I was the kid in algebra class who had trouble understanding the concept of X, and the teacher was reassuring and supportive. The tacit understanding was: *it's okay. You'll get it!*

"After experiencing the other side, she was given the choice to return. The intelligence spoke to her, but not in the verbal language of humans. She described it as beyond telepathic, more like an energetic, vibrational frequency. The 'God Energy' told her that her work on Earth would be complete if she wished, and she could enter heaven, but if she wanted to return to her physical body, she was instructed that part of her mission on Earth was to tell people about their Spirit.

"She will also focus on bringing about world peace, in part, by harnessing the power of the Divine Feminine Energy. In ancient cultures, the feminine energy was honored, and both men and women had a balance of the masculine and feminine energies. Through time, the male ego became more dominant, and the honoring of the feminine energy was lost. The Earth became a patriarchal system, but without the feminine to balance the energy of the masculine, evil erupted. There was greed for money, power, and the initiating of many wars.

"For those men and women who have forgotten the importance of balancing the masculine and feminine energy, she will reconnect them to who they really are ... with no pretending. She will teach them transformational skills that will enhance them physically, mentally, and spiritually, and they will help bring about healing and peace on our sick and troubled planet. She will be arriving tomorrow, and like you, will be asked to return in six months. You will receive more information about her, and how you will work together, after you return home."

I wondered if she looked and acted anything like Star, as well as how we were supposed to work together.

My mind shifted to the child initiate, and as it did, he responded. "The child is African American, and though she is only twelve, she has been given some very amazing abilities. You, the woman, and the child will all return and meet each other in about six months. All of you will be notified of the meeting details."

What could a child do to change the world, even a very gifted child?

"I am saving that as a surprise for when you return. You will find her quite interesting," he said.

I could feel the anxiety increasing like the red mercury rising in a thermometer on a hot summer day. *Maybe this has all been a dream, and when I wake up, I'll have a hangover because I drank too much Guinness.*

He never responded to my thoughts of doubt and instead said,

"Our next initiates have all passed the first test. They responded positively to Theophane, believing that he could do nothing for them in return. After their training and graduation, they will also be asked to sign the same book you will sign tonight. Currently, there are only three copies of the book Theophane gave you.

"Your mission will begin when you return home. At the beginning of your stay, I asked you to take daily notes that memorialized what you learned. That book, your journal, is very important, and I suggest you review it every day. Your review will keep you from falling back into unproductive habits."

He stood up, walked toward me, and motioned for me to stand. He came toward me and hugged me. I hugged him back, and when I looked at his face, he had tears in his eyes.

I was about to thank him, when he said, "The only thing that matters is kindness, and there is not enough time to do all the good things that need to be done."

He backed away, and Star walked toward me. She opened her arms and hugged me. A real hug, not the hug you give your elderly aunt on the way out the door.

When I looked in her eyes, she smiled at me, squeezed my hand, and said, "Six months will go very fast!" Then she walked toward Coach. They went into the house together, and I stood there, feeling the heat from the embers and the smell of the mesquite fire. Uncle Thomas had disappeared. I had been so involved in my discussion with Coach that I never saw him leave. I wondered what problems I'd face and reminded myself to take it a day at a time.

When I got to my room, the bed was stripped and my luggage removed. There was a note on the nightstand, which read: I brought your luggage to your car. All of us are one! Love, Star.

I looked at my watch and it read 3:15 AM. It was Sunday morning, and my flight was leaving at noon. The next initiate was due at 4:30 AM on Monday. They had a full day to prepare for her stay, and I wondered who she was, as well as who the child would be. I headed for the rented Pathfinder. The keys were in the ignition and my luggage in the back seat. I took one last look around and drove back to Phoenix. On the way, I thought about the dream that had become a nightmare and left me in a cold sweat. I knew that the responsibility facing me was overwhelming, and I took some consolation in the thought that I had six months to figure it out.

I reached the Phoenix suburbs, and the light of the new day greeted me. I decided to eat at the same restaurant I stopped at on my way to the ranch. It was breakfast time and having a juicy cheeseburger deluxe with fries, onion rings, and a Coke sounded wonderful, but when the waitress asked for my order, I answered, "A bowl of oatmeal with fruit and almonds, some well-done scrambled eggs, and a tall glass of water."

Obviously, the change had begun ... but the clock was ticking!

Epilogue

The Gifted One: the Journey Begins, is the first in a trilogy that will include: *The Gifted One: On the Road* and *The Gifted One: Going Home*. The series has been designed to introduce the reader to self-awareness and life enhancing concepts and practices in a structured, organized, and developmental manner.

It's anticipated that by the completion of the third book, if you continue reading, you will have experienced the full range of what The Gifted One has to teach. It is the intention of this series to provide instructions for living that bring about personal fulfillment, while, at the same time, providing the emotional, psychological, and inspirational tools to make the life changes needed to save the world as we know it.

Having read *The Gifted One: The Journey Begins*, you are invited to take our forty day challenge to make a change in yourself and our world. The changes can be large or small; however, we want to hear about you and, with your permission, let others know what you've accomplished.

So, forty days after you're read the book, email us at our website to let us know what you've done to transform yourself and, at the same time, our world.

In answer to the question, "Did all this really happen?" The answer is "yes and no!" It was my intention to provide information in a format that would make it memorable by providing characters and dialogue that would question, provoke, and inspire. During my research for this book, I met spiritually evolved men and women, a mystic, psychics, shamans, a very respected medicine man and a wide variety of healers. Their thoughts, actions and energy fields have been memorialized in *The Gifted One* and to all of these men and women: Namaste.

About the Author

Opportunities for presentations, life coaching and store can be found by accessing our website: andycitybear.com

Andy has his Psy.D. in School Psychology from the Graduate School of Applied and Professional Psychology, Rutgers University. He is an Associate Professor in the Special Education Department at New Jersey City University. Dr. McCabe is a life long educator and facilitated the opening of one of the first public school programs for children with autism in New Jersey. In 2010, he received the Humanitarian Award from the Simpson-Baber Foundation for Autistic Children. (www.simpson-baber.com)

Made in the USA
Middletown, DE
16 October 2017